Into the Flood

A CHRISTIAN ROMANCE
SEASONS OF FAITH BOOK 1

Milla Holt

Reinbok LIMITED

REINBOK LIMIT
London, United Kingc

Copyright © 2022 by Milla Holt

All rights reserved. No part of this publication may be reproduced, stored in a retrieval system, distributed or transmitted in any form or by any means, without prior written permission.

Published by Reinbok Limited, 111 Wolsey Drive, Kingston Upon Thames, Greater London, KT2 5DR

Publisher's Note: This is a work of fiction. Names, characters, places, and incidents are a product of the author's imagination. Locales and public names are sometimes used for atmospheric purposes. Any resemblance to actual people, living or dead, or to businesses, companies, events, institutions, or locales is completely coincidental.

Cover by 100Covers

Editing by Sara Turnquist

Into the Flood/ Milla Holt. -- 1st ed.

ISBN 978-1-913416-16-4
Print ISBN 978-1-913416-18-8

WELCOME TO THE MOSAIC COLLECTION

We are sisters, a beautiful mosaic united by the love of God through the blood of Christ.

Each month The Mosaic Collection releases one or more faith-based novels or anthologies exploring our theme, Family by His Design, and sharing stories that feature diverse, God-designed families. Stories range from mystery and women's fiction to comedic and literary fiction. We hope you'll join our Mosaic family as we explore together what truly defines a family.

If you're like us, loneliness and suffering have touched your life in ways you never imagined; but Dear One, while you may feel alone in your suffering—whatever it is—you are never alone!

Learn more about The Mosaic Collection at

www.mosaiccollectionbooks.com

Join our Reader Community, too!

www.facebook.com/groups/TheMosaicCollection

BOOKS IN THE MOSAIC COLLECTION

When Mountains Sing by Stacy Monson

Unbound by Eleanor Bertin

The Red Journal by Deb Elkink

A Beautiful Mess by Brenda S. Anderson

Hope is Born: A Mosaic Christmas Anthology

More Than Enough by Lorna Seilstad

The Road to Happenstance by Janice L. Dick

This Side of Yesterday by Angela D. Meyer

Lost Down Deep by Sara Davison

The Mischief Thief by Johnnie Alexander

Before Summer's End: Stories to Touch the Soul

Tethered by Eleanor Bertin

Calm Before the Storm by Janice L. Dick

Heart Restoration by Regina Rudd Merrick

Pieces of Granite by Brenda S. Anderson

Watercolors by Lorna Seilstad

A Star Will Rise: A Mosaic Christmas Anthology II

Eye of the Storm by Janice L. Dick

Totally Booked: A Book Lover's Companion

Lifelines by Eleanor Bertin
The Third Grace by Deb Elkink
Crazy About Maisie by Janice L. Dick
Rebuilding Joy by Regina Rudd Merrick
Song of Grace: Stories to Amaze the Soul
Written in Ink by Sara Davison
Open Circle by Stacy Monson
The Heart of Christmas: A Mosaic Christmas Anthology III
Where Hope Starts by Angela D. Meyer
Flame of Mercy by Eleanor Bertin
Through the Lettered Veil by Candace West
Broken Together by Brenda S. Anderson
Every Star in the Sky by Sara Davison
Where Healing Starts by Angela D. Meyer
All Things New: Stories to Refresh the Soul
Into the Flood by Milla Holt

Learn more at
www.mosaiccollectionbooks.com/mosaic-books

Contents

Chapter One 1
Chapter Two 21
Chapter Three 36
Chapter Four 52
Chapter Five 64
Chapter Six 73
Chapter Seven 83
Chapter Eight 92
Chapter Nine 101
Chapter Ten 110
Chapter Eleven 118
Chapter Twelve 130
Chapter Thirteen 143
Chapter Fourteen 158
Chapter Fifteen 174
Chapter Sixteen 184
Chapter Seventeen 194
Chapter Eighteen 209

Chapter Nineteen 220
Chapter Twenty 230
Chapter Twenty-One 242
Chapter Twenty-Two 261
Chapter Twenty-Three 273
Chapter Twenty-Four 290
Chapter Twenty-Five 300
Chapter Twenty-Six 317
Chapter Twenty-Seven 326
Chapter Twenty-Eight 344
Chapter Twenty-Nine 356
Chapter Thirty 363
Epilogue 373
About the Author 385

To my amazing husband, who is my number one cheerleader, and Paula and Emily who held my hand.

Chapter One

SONIA KROGSTAD WANTED ANSWERS. And, one way or another, she was going to squeeze them out of her elusive business partner today. Since Lauritz Thorsen wasn't taking her calls, she had manufactured an errand that took her to Trondheim Harbor, giving her an excuse to be in the neighborhood of his glass-fronted office building.

What could be more natural than an impromptu visit to her closest business associate? Especially since

she'd been waiting days for him to green-light a contract with their biggest investor to date. The venture capitalist was ready to put millions of dollars into Moving Up, Lauritz's groundbreaking real estate app. But if Lauritz didn't show up and close the deal, the investor would take his cash to the next shiny startup, wasting all Sonia's hard work in nurturing the lead.

She strode through the revolving glass doors, her heels clicking a fast staccato on the shiny marble floor of the lobby. The male receptionist at the front counter welcomed her with a grin, waving her toward the bank of elevators. She was a familiar enough face that the front desk staff no longer asked her to sign in for a visitor's pass.

Riding up to Lauritz's penthouse office, Sonia straightened her new Armani suit in the mirrored walls of the elevator. Maybe it stretched her budget to the limit, but the fitted tie-fastened jacket flattered her hourglass curves and went perfectly with her maroon Valentino pumps. Besides, everyone knew that cheap clothes were bad for the environment and supported sweatshops that exploited widows and children in developing countries.

Smiling at her reflection, Sonia smoothed her dark, curly bob. There was only one hairdresser in all of Trondheim she could trust with her

Afro-European hair, and he didn't come cheap.

She looked far better at forty-five than she had at twenty. After years of working hard and paying her dues, she'd come a long way from her humble small-town roots. Her days of rummaging through Salvation Army racks and bargain store discount bins were over. As a sought-after independent public relations specialist, elegant clothes and weekly salon appointments were part of her professional role.

Her well-groomed appearance was a key reason Lauritz had been eager to do business with her in the first place, along with a little flirtation on the side to make things interesting. It was a bit of fun, and who knew where it might lead?

But neither the business nor the flirtation would go anywhere unless she found out what was happening with Lauritz.

The elevator doors slid open and Sonia stepped out, slamming into a woman who was bustling past. Sheets of paper flew into the air and scattered all over the floor.

"I'm so sorry, Maria," Sonia said. The young intern, whom Sonia had seen around Lauritz's office before, gave her a strained smile, stooping to pick up the mess. Sonia allowed herself a mental fist pump. She'd once been an invisible peon at the bottom of the corporate ladder, so it gave her a kick to call even the humblest support worker by name.

Sonia's pencil skirt wasn't designed for crouching, but she did her best, angling her body downward to help Maria pick up the wayward documents.

Gathering the last of the papers, Maria smiled again. "Thank you. I'm sorry about that."

"It wasn't your fault. I should have been looking where I was going. See you soon."

Maria scurried down the hallway and Sonia stepped through the office door and into pure bedlam.

Normally humming with contained, efficient energy, today Lauritz's business HQ resembled an ants' nest after a collision with a bulldozer. Workers scrambled back and forth. The ringing of telephones filled the air, but no one appeared to be answering the calls.

One man, sweat ringing the armpits of his blue shirt, stood next to a heavy-duty paper shredder, feeding it from a pile of documents that teetered at the edge of his desk. The papers slid to the floor and he barked out a string of profanities.

What was going on? Sonia headed to the desk where the receptionist, Rita, stood.

The petite woman's face was flushed, her normally pristine blond hair slipping out of its bun. The phone on her desk was ringing, but instead of answering it, Rita stuffed a handful of papers into the churning metal blades of a shredder. Her pale eyes widened as she looked up at Sonia. "How did you get up here?"

Sonia stared back at her. How was she supposed to answer such a weird question? She gestured over her shoulder. "With the elevator."

"Past the lobby reception? They were under instructions not to send any visitors up today."

"I'm not really a visitor, though. I work with Lauritz."

Rita fidgeted with her stack of papers, her hands skittering over them like a pair of flighty squirrels. "Nobody other than on-site staff was supposed to come up here today. We're really busy, as you can see."

Sonia glanced at the chaos surrounding them. "I can see that. But since I'm here now, could I have a quick word with Lauritz? I won't be more than five minutes."

"Mr. Thorsen isn't in." Rita picked up another handful of papers and slid the edges into the shredder.

Sonia looked past the receptionist to Lauritz's closed office door. "He's not in, or just unavailable?"

"He's not in," Rita repeated, her gaze sliding away from Sonia's face. "Why don't you call and make an appointment?"

"Can't you set up the appointment now?"

"That's not possible. Company policy states that we can only make appointments over the phone. It really would be better if you called."

Sonia pointed at the shrilling phone lying between them on the desk. "You mean like these people who are trying to call right now?"

Rita glared at her, face flushed.

Sonia took a slow, calming breath. Time to try honey instead of vinegar.

Smiling, she injected as much sweetness into her tone as she could muster. “I can see you’re really busy, and I don’t want to add to your workload. But since I’m here now, how about you schedule me in and save me the trouble of calling for an appointment?”

“That’s not possible. I already told you I can only make appointments over the phone.”

“Since when has that been a policy?” So much for being syrupy sweet.

“Since we realized that drop-in visitors disrupt everyone’s workflow,” Rita snapped. “Now, if you don’t mind, I have a lot to do. Have a nice day.”

Sonia bit back a sharp retort. Squabbling with the receptionist would get her nowhere. Glancing at Lauritz's closed door, she sighed and half-turned to leave.

A harried-looking man balancing a stack of ledgers knocked on the door, then stepped inside. He closed the door behind him, but not before Sonia glimpsed a pale faced, unshaven Lauritz sitting hunched at his gleaming glass and steel desk.

Sonia whirled back to Rita. "I thought you said Lauritz wasn't in."

Color flooded Rita's face. "I—I'm under strict instructions not to let anyone in. It'll cost me my job if you go in there."

So Lauritz *was* avoiding her. The sneaky, cowardly, lying weasel. Something strange and stinky was going on. Sonia could walk away and avoid an awkward confrontation, but she had an important investor waiting for answers. No way was she leaving until Lauritz spoke to her.

"I'll tell him you tried to stop me," she said, stepping around Rita's desk.

Rita dropped her papers and held her hands up, her blue eyes wide. "Please don't go in there."

"I need to see him." Sonia walked toward Lauritz's door.

"I'll call security."

Sonia looked over her shoulder.

Rita, jaw set, clutched a phone receiver in a death-like grip.

Sonia held her gaze and was dimly aware of a hush around them, as though everyone else in the room held their breath.

Rita broke eye contact first, turning to the phone keypad. She punched in three digits. "Hello, security? I need someone up at Thorsen Solutions to remove an unwelcome guest."

"Fine. I'm going." Sonia gritted her teeth. Getting thrown out of the building would consummate her humiliation. She gathered the threadbare remains of her dignity, held her head high, and stalked toward the door, staring down the blue-shirted man next to the big paper shredder.

He ducked his head as she swept past.

She faced the elevator doors, her ears burning. Lauritz had better have a sterling explanation, delivered along with a groveling apology. Besides all the investors she had brought to him over the past months, she had liquidated her pension fund and sunk it all buying into Lauritz's startup. Her nest egg probably paid the salary of that receptionist who'd just called security on her.

Somebody jostled her elbow and Sonia looked up. Maria, the intern, hovered in front of her, arms loaded

with document folders. "Sorry, I'm so clumsy today. Goodbye."

Maria turned to leave, but as she brushed past, she pressed a folded scrap of paper into Sonia's hand.

The elevator doors slid open, and Sonia stepped inside. As the doors closed, she unfolded the paper Maria had given her. It was a note.

There's something you need to know. Meet me at the Java Bean Café down the street in ten minutes.

Her heart thumping, Sonia crumpled the note and stuffed it into her handbag.

Sonia sat in the Java Bean Café, staring at her phone while her cup of black coffee cooled. As she waited for Maria, she clicked through Lauritz's business website and scoured his social media accounts. No mention of anything out of the ordinary. But the vibe at Thorsen Solutions was way off. They were hiding something big. Something way bigger than just Lauritz holed up in his office.

She checked the time. Ten minutes had passed, but Maria still wasn't here. She'd give her ten more minutes, and then put in a call to her lawyer.

As the clock crawled past the five-minute mark, Maria rushed through the doors and approached Sonia's table near the window. She walked

past, murmuring, "Please move to the back of the café. We're too conspicuous near the window."

Feeling like Norway's answer to 007, Sonia gathered up her coffee and purse and followed Maria to a secluded booth at the back of the crowded café.

Maria scanned the room and leaned forward. "I only have five minutes, so I'll make it brief. You've always been kind to me, which is why I'm going to tell you this."

She looked over her shoulder and lowered her voice. "You need to distance yourself as far as you can from Lauritz. Something big is going down. The police are involved, and I think Interpol is, too. This morning, Lauritz gave orders to shred a bunch of documents, and everyone's hard drives were to be wiped. I think it's only a matter of time before they arrest him. You're a decent person and judging from the way they're stopping you from seeing him, I'm sure you're not a part of whatever shady deals have been going on. If I were you, I'd get out as fast as you can."

Each of Maria's words hit Sonia with the force of a sledgehammer. "Are you sure?"

"Trust me. The Titanic has hit the iceberg, and it's sinking. I know you've invested a chunk of money with Lauritz. Get it out if you can. I'll be leaving as soon as I'm done with

my shift today. I'm sorry I couldn't do more for you." Maria glanced at her watch and stood. "I'd better go. I don't want anyone to know I've been speaking with you."

Sonia watched her leave. Around her table, the café bustled along as usual, as though Sonia's world hadn't just spun off its axis.

Chapter Two

AXEL VIKHAMMER NURSED HIS third cup of hospital vending machine coffee, dredging his mind for any scrap of wisdom on how to parent his only child.

He came up empty.

Teenage daughters should come with a user manual. Then he could look up the chapter titled, “What to do when child’s best friend self-harms” and he’d know how to be the kind of father Karla needed.

He could get a clue about whether allowing a thirteen-year-old to visit her emotionally fragile friend in the hospital was the right thing to do. And maybe pick up some befitting words of comfort. He'd pay hard cash for a primer on how to talk to Karla about anything and get more than a monosyllabic response.

He stood and paced the windowless waiting area deep in the bowels of Havdal Hospital, staring down the hall toward the patient rooms. The already drab colors of the walls looked even more washed out under the fluorescent lighting. Did all hospitals shop at the same paint supplier for this lifeless shade of beige?

Karla should be back any minute now after visiting her friend. What could she and Erin have been talking about over the past hour?

Teenage females were a species alien to Axel's world. Which made it ironic that God had dropped one into his life. His daughter. They shared genetic material, but Karla was a stranger to him. He hadn't known she existed until less than a year ago, shortly before she came to live with him. And now it was up to him to raise her into a well-adjusted human being.

The responsibility weighed on him, dominating his worries and prayers. Her wellbeing mattered more than anything else, but he could never tell

whether or not he was doing the right thing.

He was already floundering over the most basic issues, like how much of a weekly allowance she should get, and now he had to help Karla cope with a self-harming friend whose cry for help had landed her in the hospital.

Computers were so much easier to deal with than people. He could break down the most complex coding problem into logical sequences and loops. But interacting with his daughter felt like they were mumbling different languages at each other through a thick wall of Plexiglas.

And it wasn't just because she'd grown up in Southern Norway and spoke a different dialect than what was common here in the north. He rather liked her accent with its soft r's and regional colloquialisms. When she spoke to him at all.

A door opened halfway down the hall and Karla stepped out. She trudged toward the reception, a slight figure in black leggings and an oversized sweatshirt. It still shocked him how much she resembled him, with her wavy almost-black hair and dark blue eyes. He hadn't needed to take a paternity test, despite his lawyer's advice. He knew in his core that Karla was his child.

She headed to the water dispenser in the corner of the room. Keeping her back to Axel, she downed a drink of

water and tossed the empty cup into the recycling bin.

Axel binned his coffee cup. "Are you ready to go home?"

"Yeah."

They walked in silence through a maze of hallways, following the yellow line that marked the way out of the hospital. They made it to the parking lot and into Axel's silver Ford Kuga without exchanging another word, while Axel sifted through and discarded a dozen potential conversation starters.

Buckling his seatbelt, he finally settled on asking, "Is Erin okay?"

"She's alive." Karla clasped her hands between her knees.

Silence settled again as he navigated onto the highway. Karla stared out of the passenger window as the coastal scenery slipped past. All the winter snow was gone now, and the region was in the full grip of Norway's short but dramatic spring. It would take forty-five minutes to drive around the fjord to get back home to Berghaven. The town was too small to have a traffic light, never mind a hospital.

Thank God he ran his software development business from home and could drop everything to bring Karla to Havdal.

Axel's hand moved toward the radio dial. Music or a talk radio station would break the wall of quiet. But that might imply to Karla that he didn't want to talk. And nothing could be further from the truth.

He withdrew his hand, placing it back on the steering wheel, and throwing a quick glance at his daughter. He wanted to connect with her, to have a meaningful conversation. Most of all, he longed to know what lay behind those unreadable blue eyes that looked so much like his. "Are you hungry?"

She shrugged, folding her arms tighter across her chest.

"I thought we could have Chinese tonight," he said.

"Chinese sounds good."

His stock of conversational topics worn out, Axel focused on the road.

What was going through Karla's head? Her best friend had just tried to commit suicide. With all the hours the girls spent together, had the topic ever come up? An icy shard pierced his chest. Had Karla ever thought of doing something like that? He did his best for her. He prayed daily for her, took her to church, kept a regular routine at home. But was that enough?

Thankfully, Erin had made it and was getting the help she needed. But seeing Karla's friend do something so

drastic froze Axel to the core. His daughter had already been through so much in her short life. Losing her mother, then being sprung on a father who hadn't known he had a daughter.

And now her best friend had come close to ending her life. These were the nightmares that kept him up at night—fears that Karla might slip into self-harm or substance abuse. Her mother had been self-destructive. Who knew what Karla had been through growing up?

As the miles slipped past, he repeated the same words he'd prayed so often. The ones he said as soon as he woke up and as he drifted off to sleep every night. *Lord, protect my daughter. Help me be a good father to her. Lead her to you, the best Father of all.*

As they drove into Berghaven, Axel brightened at the sight of the Community Arts Center, the one place he knew for sure Karla enjoyed going. She dragged herself to school, and she tolerated church, but she thrived at the Arts Center.

“Don’t you have a painting workshop today?” he asked.

Karla shot him a glance. “Classes are canceled today. The Center is closing.”

Axel stared at her, then remembered he was driving. He turned his eyes back to the road in time to avoid colliding with a lamp post. "What do you mean, the Center is closing?"

Karla reached inside her backpack and pulled out a crumpled letter. "It's all here." She set it on the dashboard.

Axel steered into the parking lot of the Golden Dragon Chinese restaurant and picked up the letter, a circular sent to all the regular users of the Berghaven Community Arts Center.

It is with deep regret that we announce the closure of the Center. This is not a decision we take lightly, given how many people are blessed by the work we do. Despite an extensive search, we cannot find a buyer for the premises and no longer have the

funding to continue operations. Thank you so much for the support you've given us over the years, and we trust that God will continue to help you flourish in the gift and talent he has given you.

Axel looked at Karla. "I'm sorry if you told me this and it didn't register."

"I didn't tell you. It came up at the same time as that stuff with Erin, so I had other things on my mind."

He folded up the letter. This was yet another blow for Karla. And he'd not known anything about it until now. What kind of father did that make him? He reached into his wallet and extracted a couple of two hundred kroner notes, handing the money to

Karla. "Why don't you go in and order some food to go? Order what you like and make it enough for two."

Karla went inside the restaurant and Axel reread the letter. How could the Arts Center be closing? Working from home, he was always the last to find out things others had known about for months. But this was huge.

He vaguely remembered leaflets floating around about fund-raising and plans to sell the Center's building, an important community hub. He had not realized the Arts Center was in such dire straits. Founded as a Christian non-profit, the Center didn't receive any public funds but relied only on donations or whatever money it could generate.

Karla and Erin hung out there a lot, along with other teenagers from the area. It was a safe place for them to nurture their creativity in several branches of the arts.

The Center ran painting and pottery classes, a community choir, and a mother and baby group. What would happen to all these people if it closed? Berghaven had nothing else like it.

He pulled out his phone. He had some money saved, thanks to the sale of his first startup company. First thing tomorrow, he'd call his accountant. He was going to need to release a sizeable chunk of funding. He could not let the Center close.

3

Chapter Three

THE FALLOUT FROM LAURITZ'S arrest was not as bad as Sonia had feared. It was worse.

Maria's warning in the café a week ago had prepared her to expect something big. Now, the afternoon after the news hit, Sonia scrambled with the aftermath, making as much progress as if she were shoring up a disintegrating sandcastle at high tide. Rattled and bewildered herself, she paced her home office fielding the latest in an hours-long stream of phone calls from scared and angry business associates.

Moving Up, a real estate platform meant to disrupt the property market, turned out to be little more than a pyramid scheme. It was now crashing and burning, and incinerating Sonia's life savings, career, and professional reputation as it blew up.

Instead of running an actual business, Lauritz had used the funds of newer investors to pay off older ones. Despite the fancy website, slick app, and all the promo material and social media buzz Sonia had helped create, there was no Moving Up. It was all a front that allowed Lauritz to take people's money.

“This scam has cost me three quarters of a million kroner,” Mikkel Giske, a former business associate, screamed into her ear.

At least he got off lightly. When Sonia finished tallying her losses, she would be lucky to have burned anything under two million. Her pension fund was all gone, not to mention the additional money she’d borrowed against her condo.

“I trusted you, Sonia,” Mikkel said. “And I trusted Lauritz. How could you let this happen?”

“Believe me, I’m more sorry than you know. I did my best.” Sonia’s voice was hoarse after hours talking on the phone. “I followed all due diligence. I believed in Lauritz so much that I invested some of my own money, which I've also lost."

Mikkel was not interested in anyone else's sob story. "This is going to cost me a partnership. I recommended that my company and colleagues buy shares in Moving Up. And thanks to you, I look like an idiot. Is there any way we can get our money back?"

"I don't know," Sonia said. "The best thing for you would be to contact a securities fraud lawyer and get their advice."

Her own lawyer had not been encouraging about Sonia's chances of clawing back her investment. Worse still, he'd told Sonia that her primary

worry ought to be ensuring she wasn't implicated in the fraud along with Lauritz. Otherwise, she might find herself getting sued by swindled investors.

Mikkel was still ranting. His words stung, but Sonia gritted her teeth against the onslaught.

Her gaze drifted to her computer. Her email inbox overflowed with messages that were the electronic equivalent of Mikkel's diatribe from people who, on her recommendation, had invested in Moving Up.

Satisfied with fully venting his spleen, Mikkel hung up. Sonia put her phone down and massaged her temples. These calls were sucking away her will to live. Her head ached, her throat was sore, and she had nothing to say that these angry people wanted to hear.

But what else was she supposed to do? She couldn't leave them hanging without the best explanation she could give. Not when all of them were in this mess because she'd encouraged them to go into business with Lauritz.

She sat at her desk to deal with her emails, copying and pasting the form response she was giving all of them: ***I am no longer employed by or associated with Moving Up or Thorsen Solutions. Please address all correspondence to the Thorsen Solutions head office.***

But severing her formal connection with Lauritz couldn't erase the mud that clung to her name. There was no question of finding another client in Trondheim or, indeed, in any Norwegian city, after her collaboration with Lauritz. She had done too good a job for him—raising his profile, making investors know, like, and trust him, and put their money in his Ponzi scheme.

And there was also the personal betrayal. But, no. She wasn't going there. She grappled her thoughts away from contemplating the candlelit dinners and flirty emails. Professional humiliation was bad enough without admitting the hopes she'd once entertained about where her relationship with Lauritz might go.

The phone rang again and Sonia picked it up, bracing herself for another earful of abuse. But the caller ID showed Lisa Meland, her best friend from her hometown of Berghaven.

Sonia hit the answer button. "Lisa! It's great to hear from you."

"Hi. I was just thinking about you and decided to call."

Great. The news about her career disaster had hit Berghaven now. "Any reason in particular why I'm on your mind?"

"I saw a story about Lauritz in the newspaper and I thought maybe you could use a friend."

Sonia's eyes filled up. She hadn't spoken to Lisa in months beyond the occasional text message. And yet Lisa was reaching out to her.

When Sonia had mentioned what she was going through to her closest circle in Trondheim, their responses had gone along the lines of, "It must be terrible being you. Let us know how it turns out. Bye!"

She dabbed at her eyes. She'd been able to hold it together until now. But hearing a friendly voice made the tears leak out. "Thank you. It means a lot that you called."

"So, what exactly is happening?"

She filled Lisa in on the criminal charges pending against Lauritz and all her other clients bailing on her. "I won't be able to keep up on my mortgage at this rate. I borrowed against the condo and cashed in my pension fund to invest with Lauritz. It's a good thing my estate agent is the only person in Trondheim who's still speaking to me because I need to sell this place."

"Maybe it's a blessing in disguise that Lauritz scammed you along with everyone else."

Sonia frowned. "What do you mean?"

"Won't that prove to people that you weren't part of his scheme? If you can show you got swindled as well, they can't come after you for luring them in."

"I hadn't thought of that. You know, that's the most hopeful thing I've heard all day. Thank you." Sonia blew her nose and tossed the wadded up tissue at a waste basket, missing by several feet. Her aim was as sketchy as her judgement of character.

"You're welcome. And since you're thinking of selling your condo and moving, would you be open to taking a job here in Berghaven?"

Lisa had gone from making sense to throwing out ludicrous suggestions.

Sonia had left Berghaven over twenty-five years ago. Growing up poor, and sick of being the object of pity in her church community, she'd left her home town determined to make a name for herself in the city.

The thought of returning as a failure galled Sonia so much that she could taste the bitterness in the back of her throat. "Work in Berghaven? I don't think—"

"Hear me out," Lisa interrupted. "There's a guy I know from church. He's a businessman. Some kind of tech genius who invented a productivity app."

Sonia's grip tightened on her phone. "Really, Lisa? Do PR for another start-

up? I'm still reeling from the last time I was involved with promoting a whiz-bang app, remember?"

"The job isn't with his startup. He recently bought the Berghaven Community Arts Center, but it's a bit of a money pit. He needs someone who can help with the fund-raising."

"Why would a businessman in software development want to buy a non-profit arts center?"

"I'm not sure, to be honest," Lisa said. "Maybe he's got a long-range money-spinning idea for it. Or perhaps he just didn't want it to have to close its doors. But, anyway, he says it's going to carry on as usual and remain separate from his other business."

Sonia sighed. She looked around her office, recently remodeled so it could look good as a backdrop to her social media video content. A remodel she was still paying for. Her gaze fell on her email inbox with rows of messages heralding the demise of her career.

A potential job opening, even in Berghaven, beat staying unemployed in Trondheim.

"I'm listening," Sonia said.

"That's as much as I know right now. Why don't you polish up your resume, and I'll tell him you might be interested? Even if you don't want to

try for the job, you could always stay with me while things settle down and you figure out what to do next."

Sonia's heart warmed. "That's a very kind offer."

"Please say you'll come, then?"

"I'll seriously consider it. Clients aren't exactly beating down my door. Or, rather, they are beating down my door, but with their torches and pitchforks. So, yes, your proposal is on a very short list of options I have right now."

Lisa laughed. "Not quite a ringing acceptance, but I'll take it."

"So, how are you getting on? How's Eline doing at the university?"

Lisa sighed. "She's okay, apart from some boyfriend drama."

"Ugh, that's the worst."

"Tell me about it."

They talked a bit more about their friends in Berghaven. As usual, they skirted around any mention of Lisa's estranged husband.

Sonia glanced at her watch. Time to get back to putting out fires. If it was possible to douse a forest fire with a water pistol. "Thanks so much for calling and for your offer. But I'd better get back to work. I'll be in touch soon."

Chapter Four

AFTER BUYING THE BERGHAVEN Community Arts Center in haste, Axel now had plenty of time to repent at leisure.

The surprised delight on his daughter Karla's face when she heard the Arts Center would stay open almost made up for the harsh reality of what it would take to keep the place functioning.

Against his financial manager's advice, he had met with the Center's board and hammered out a deal which involved his purchasing the building and contracting the former staff members to run it and continue their services seamlessly.

But the Center was hemorrhaging money and unless Axel plugged the holes and made it self-supporting, it would soon bleed him dry.

He needed to hire a fund-raiser urgently and he and Erna Vigeland, the Center's director, now waited to interview the only qualified candidate for the job.

Axel scanned the resume in front of him. Although she came on Lisa's recommendation, he had major misgivings about Sonia Krogstad.

Sonia may have grown up in Berghaven, but she was only back in town because her big city career had hit the skids. Would she bail out at the first opportunity? Still, he had promised Lisa that he would give her friend a hearing. At least then he could say he had met Sonia, and she was a poor fit.

The door to Erna's office opened and a tall, dark-skinned woman walked in. She gleamed with urbanite polish, from her stylishly cut hair down to her razor-sharp high heels made for stepping out of limousines and onto city pavements.

Smiling, she walked forward with a hand stretched toward Erna. Axel stared at her sparkly, bejeweled nails.

How could a person do anything practical with nails that long?

"Pleased to meet you. I'm Sonia Krogstad."

Erna grasped Sonia's hand and greeted her enthusiastically. "I'm so glad you could come. How was your trip from Trondheim?"

"Not bad. It doesn't seem to have changed very much since my last visit. Did you know I grew up here?"

Axel crossed his arms. Berghaven might be her hometown, but Sonia's warm, husky voice had lost the lilting tones of the northern dialect.

Erna nodded with vigor. "We heard that. When did you leave?"

"At least twenty-five years ago." Sonia tilted her head to the side and giggled. "I won't get any more detailed than that because it makes me feel old."

Erna laughed. "That was before my husband and I moved here. It's wonderful to have someone local interested in the job, especially with all the experience you have. Maybe some of your big city success will rub off on us."

Did Axel imagine it, or did Sonia's smile falter? But it was soon back at full beam.

"I remember the Center from way back, so it was a very interesting prospect," she said.

How interesting would it be if her career was still on track? She'd probably not give a job like this a second thought.

Sonia faced Axel, a wave of a fresh floral perfume wafting off the hand she extended to him. "Axel Vikhammer, I presume. Lovely to meet you."

He took her hand. Her grip was like a steel gauntlet cloaked in velvet. A power handshake. "Thanks for coming," he said. "I'll let Erna take the lead. She's the expert on the Center."

Erna gestured toward the door. "Why don't we take you on a brief tour of the place so you can get a feel for what we do?"

Sonia grinned. "That would be wonderful! Let's go."

Axel followed the women as Erna led the way. They made an interesting contrast. Erna, wearing flat shoes and a plain sweater, barely came up to Sonia's shoulder. Sonia's impeccably tailored royal blue business suit flattered her curves, and her three-inch heels extended her already considerable height even further. He was 5'10", but if he stood next to her, Axel wasn't sure whether she wouldn't be the taller one.

Erna looked up at Sonia. "It's mid-morning on a Tuesday, so the Center isn't at its busiest. Things get hopping in the afternoon with the children's and teens' activities and the community choir. But right now we have a pottery workshop which mainly our senior citizens attend. And just over here—" She gestured into a room on their right — "is one of my favorite sessions of all. Adults with intellectual disabilities get to try out different types of art. Today they're painting ceramics."

Sonia peeked through the windowed door. "That looks like so much fun. I remember painting my own mug. I kept it for ages until I dropped it and it broke."

As they toured the Center, Sonia's enthusiasm only climbed. She gushed over the ceramics class and cooed at the tots in the mother and baby group. Was all that intensity genuine? What

could she see in this place to get her all fired up?

"There is so much potential here." Sonia waved her glitter-tipped hands around as she stood in the middle of the run-down cafeteria, a designer-shod foot resting on one of hundreds of cracks on the linoleum floor. "I could see a dozen ways of bringing in potential revenue. I'm sure there are several businesses who would be willing to give back to this place. There are also some public grants you might be interested in pursuing."

"Really?" Erna glanced at Axel. "We haven't sought public funding because the Center is founded on Christian traditions. Although we're not affiliated with any particular church, we promote Christian principles. Being self-financed allows us to preserve our independence. We were worried that taking a government grant would open us to influences we may not necessarily agree with."

Axel crossed his arms. "The Center's ethos remains the same. We don't want any public grants."

"Fair enough." Sonia shrugged her shoulders. "Even taking that off the table, there's still a lot you could do to raise funds. There are private charity foundations who also give grants. You could approach the local chamber of commerce, or individual businessmen. There's also the potential to do your own income-generating activities. Themed

birthday parties, like ceramic painting or pottery-making parties. T-shirt printing... The sky really is the limit."

Erna nodded eagerly, her eyes glowing.

Axel frowned. This Sonia might be full of ideas, but what was really motivating her? "You seem very well-versed in charity fund-raising."

She faced him with the full blast of her smile. "I cut my PR teeth on charity fund-raising and I don't think I'd be tooting my horn if I said I've had significant success. This is the kind of work I find most personally rewarding."

"Is that so?" Axel fixed his gaze on her brown eyes. "Then why were you mixed up with Lauritz Thorsen?"

Chapter Five

"Excuse me?" Sonia stared at Axel. Had this man really gone there?

Arms crossed, his blue eyes locked on hers. He asked again, "With your long pedigree of involvement in charity fund-raising, why were you mixed up with Lauritz Thorsen?"

Her ears weren't playing tricks. He was going for the jugular. But she had nothing to hide and hadn't done anything criminal or shameful. Bring it on. She raised her chin. "Moving Up appeared to be an innovative and useful app. I was excited about making it known to the wider community and giving businesspeople a chance to invest in an exciting product that would help and also be financially rewarding."

"Financially rewarding," he echoed, the smirk on his lips the first smile he'd worn since she got here. "I suppose it was rewarding. Just not for the investors who responded to your pitch."

Sonia was over this needling from Axel. But at least he was finally being open with his hostility. That was way better than the silent and unsettling

waves of disapproval that had rolled off him ever since she'd walked in.

Placing one hand on her hip, she didn't break eye contact. "I was also an investor in Moving Up. I was one of the first to put down funding and I'll be one of the last in line to recover any losses. I backed Lauritz Thorsen because I believed in his app. I never take on a job I don't believe in."

She held his gaze, refusing to blink first.

Erna swept into the charged silence, her hands fluttering. "Shall we go into the art gallery? I would love to hear your opinion on the pieces, Sonia. Some of them are truly extraordinary."

Sonia turned away from Axel and smiled at Erna. “Yes, of course. I’ve been looking forward to seeing the gallery.” This job interview had gone down the toilet, but Erna was a sweet, genuine lady. It wasn’t her fault her boss lacked any sense of courtesy.

They left the cafeteria and walked across the hall into a large space. Sonia itched to glance over her shoulder to check whether Axel had come with them, but held the temptation at bay. Her chances of landing the job were dead, embalmed, and buried. Had she ever stood a chance of getting hired? Judging by Axel’s frosty behavior from the get-go, he’d made his mind up before the interview began. But she could still be polite to Erna and

browse the gallery before going back to Lisa's place and resuming her job hunt.

Sonia walked to a large canvas on the wall, determined to find something positive to say about the painting, no matter how amateurish the artwork. Her low expectations vanished as she took in the well-executed oil painting, a stunning image of the harbor in Berghavensfjord. "Did one of the Center's clients paint this?"

"Yes, indeed." Erna preened like a proud mother hen. "Every piece on display in this gallery was created by somebody who used our Arts Center."

The door behind them opened. Twisting around, Sonia glimpsed Axel stepping in. She turned her back on him and focused on Erna's chatter.

The older woman pointed at a watercolor portrait of a dog. "This one was painted when the artist, Mariamu Kotto, was just eleven years old. She came to Norway as a refugee and the integration department settled her and her parents in Berghaven. She's studying art at the University of Bergen now, and we couldn't be prouder."

They moved on to the next picture. Sonia sensed Axel's brooding presence as he stood by the door.

"This piece over here..." Erna pointed at an abstract ceramic sculpture of a couple sitting side by side. "The gentleman who made it only took up this art form after his retirement. He used to be a regular here at the Center and came to a ceramics workshop we held. He made this when he was eighty, and his family was kind enough to let us keep it after he passed."

Sonia didn't have to feign admiration. As she listened to Erna, it became easier to ignore Axel. The artwork was lovely. A surprising number of the budding artists had developed their talent thanks to the Center's resources. For each of the outstanding artists whose work was displayed, how many other people had simply found joy dabbling in a rewarding hobby the Center allowed them to explore?

The place was doing good work. It was a pity she wouldn't be able to help them continue. It was also too bad because she really needed this job. Ah, well. Back to the drawing board. She had a couple more places she needed to send her resume.

As they rounded the full circuit of the gallery, Sonia spoke to Erna. "Thank you for taking me around. I enjoyed seeing what you do here, and I wish you all the best."

As they shook hands, Erna's gaze flickered to Axel, who still stood next to the door.

Sonia straightened the strap of her purse over her shoulder and faced Axel. "I'll be on my way now. Thanks for the opportunity."

Axel uncrossed his arms and placed his fists on his hips. "The job is yours if you want it. When will you be able to start?"

6

Chapter Six

IF SO MUCH HADN'T been on the line, Axel might have laughed at Sonia's wide-eyed, gaping-mouthed shock. His job offer appeared to have struck her speechless. Erna, too, stared at him.

A smile tugged at his lips as he repeated, "If you want it, the job is yours."

Erna recovered her brain-to-mouth connection first, clasping her hands together. "That's wonderful, Axel. I'm

fully on board with your decision. I hope you'll consider coming to work with us, Sonia."

Sonia blinked rapidly. "Thank you. I admit I wasn't really expecting... But thank you."

He took the hand she held out, struck again by the strength of her grip. Was that what she was like? A core of steel in an elegant, beautiful package? A smart, sophisticated woman like her must be scraping the bottom of the barrel to take a job in a no-name arts center in a small backwater town. It told him one thing, though. If she was as shady as Lauritz Thorsen, she wouldn't be here in Berghaven hustling for the kind of work Axel could offer.

Releasing her hand, he said, "Although I own this building, I've contracted Erna and her team to manage things here. This is not my normal line of business, and the Arts Center isn't connected in any way to my other affairs. I'm not involved in the day-to-day running of this place, but it's vitally important that it covers its own costs. So, I'll keep a close eye on your efforts to make that happen."

Erna swept in before Sonia could respond. "This is so exciting! I just know you're going to help us turn things around. At our morning prayer meeting today, I was telling everyone..."

As Erna talked, Axel's gaze strayed to a charcoal and ink profile of a

woman framed on the far wall of the gallery. Karla had drawn the portrait of her mother shortly after moving to Berghaven. She spent hours sketching in her notepads and attended every available art workshop and class here, but the portrait was the only piece of Karla's work he'd seen. Although non-verbal and not directed at him, it was also the only reference to her mother he'd witnessed.

As always, when looking at the sketch, he had to wrestle past his resentment of the woman in the portrait and focus on his daughter's talent. Karla needed the Arts Center. He couldn't let it close. Even if she plastered every surface with images of her mother.

He shifted his gaze to Sonia, wishing he had the discernment to measure her intentions and weigh her mindset. He'd prayed for someone to help with fund-raising, and she was the only candidate who had anything close to the skill set required for the job. Despite his misgivings about her, he'd have to trust that she was God's provision for his current need.

"Many people depend on the Arts Center." The way Sonia and Erna's heads whipped around to face him told Axel he'd just spoken his thoughts aloud and interrupted their conversation.

Sonia nodded. "I'm aware of that."

His face burned, but he decided to complete his thought. "I don't mean just the livelihoods of those who staff it, but the clients who use it—the teens, the retirees, the mothers who come here with their babies. This place means a lot to Berghaven. Do you understand that?"

"I grew up here," Sonia said. "I was once a teen in this town who needed an outlet. I know what the Center means, and I'll do my best for it."

Axel inclined his head. "In that case, I'll email you a job offer and a contract. I expect great things from you."

Ten minutes later, sitting in her parked car, Sonia pulled out her phone and punched in Lisa's number.

Lisa answered straight away. "How'd it go?"

"I got the job."

"That's fantastic! I knew they'd be insane not to hire you."

"That's what I thought before the interview. But for a while there, things looked a bit dicey. I didn't think that friend of yours wanted to work with me. What's up with him, anyway?"

"Who, Axel?" Lisa asked. "What do you mean?"

"He had this attitude right from the moment I got in. He was barely

courteous and hardly said anything most of the time. When he finally opened his mouth, he all but accused me of being in on Lauritz's scam."

"Really? What did you say?"

"I told him I'd been swindled, too. I don't really remember what else I said, but by then I was done. I'd checked out mentally because I thought, what's the point? He's not going to hire me. And then, out of the blue, he tells me the job is mine. The other lady doing the interview was as shocked as I was. Is he always that weird?"

"I wouldn't say he's weird," Lisa said. "He's not exactly chatty and keeps to himself most of the time. You know the type, one of those guys at church who's not out there making noise but helps out quietly when things need doing. I've always thought he was a nice enough guy, although hard to get to know. He's been a regular at church for about ten years, but it's only when I worked with him on a couple of committees that we got to talking a bit more. We all think it was wonderful of him to step in and save the Arts Center."

"He said he's going to keep a close eye on my work. Maybe I'll get to see some of that wonderfulness up close."

Lisa laughed. "Congratulations, though! I hope that means you'll stick around for a while."

"Thanks." Sonia had missed Lisa, and living with her friend was fun. But she'd only stay here as long as it took to get the Arts Center on its feet. Then, having done her good deed for the town, she could wave goodbye to Berghaven and Axel Vikhammer and move on to bigger and better things.

Chapter Seven

SONIA PLUCKED A STRAND of slimy, cold spaghetti off her silk blouse, forcing herself to smile at the toddler, who was still flinging handfuls of rainbow-colored noodles all around himself.

Exactly one month ago, she'd been at a glitzy red-carpet event in Oslo, rubbing shoulders with an award-winning playwright, multimillionaire entrepreneurs, and high-ranking public officials. Now, she sat in the

mother and baby group that met at the Berghaven Community Arts Center, an easy target for flying pasta, praying the food coloring on the spaghetti wouldn't stain her top. Why had she chosen to join this table with the hyper toddler when, on the other side of the room, another lady sat with a mellow baby?

"Haakon, darling, why don't you try to make a big spaghetti mountain instead of throwing it around?" The child's mother successfully redirected his energy, allowing Sonia to remove all the remaining pasta from her lap.

She inched her chair backward to be out of range in case Haakon decided to hurl spaghetti again.

If she avoided brooding over the huge climbdown in her circumstances, her first week at work here was going reasonably well. She'd sat in on as many activities as she could, getting a feel for how the community used the place. And it turned out that the Center did a lot more than she'd thought.

Haakon's mother, Marit, stroked her son's wispy blond hair. "I was so relieved Mr. Vikhammer bought the Center. We were gutted to hear it was going to close."

"So, you'd say it has an important place in your life?" Sonia asked.

"It's a lifesaver! Haakon is my first child, and I felt really isolated until we found out about this place. We come here every Tuesday and Thursday. It's made such a difference to us." She looked at her child and bit her lip. "We don't have a lot of extra money to spend on activities, so this is a great chance for Haakon and me to learn about low-cost things we can do. I'd never have thought he could have so much fun with just pasta."

Haakon pushed the colored spaghetti around, his face a picture of intense concentration. He was kind of cute when he wasn't throwing pasta around.

Marit looked up. "Do you have any children?"

"No." With Sonia's forty-fifth birthday a distant dot in the rearview mirror and no relationship prospects in sight, it was increasingly unlikely she'd ever have a baby of her own. Never mind babies. She was old enough to be Marit's mother. The thought depressed her, so she stuffed it into the crowded mental closet where she shoved all the things she didn't want to think about.

Her top priority right now wasn't marriage or babies. It was paying off her debts and rebuilding her retirement fund. Her job here paid enough to get by month to month, but nowhere near what she hoped to earn to meet her long-term goals. Still, it

beat being unemployed. And at least she was doing something worthwhile.

Like the other things the Center did, this mother and baby group was worthy but low key. She could help them find funding, but it was going to be behind-the-scenes work. Not exactly the kind of job in which she could make a big splash and raise her profile again. But she would do right by these people.

If she was to make any headway with this fund-raising plan, she had to involve the people who used the Center. Donors loved to have a human face attached to their charitable causes. Maybe with all the mucus washed off, Haakon would be cute and presentable enough to take part in a photo shoot as part of the publicity campaign. She'd have to ask Marit and the other parents if they'd consent to pictures of their children being used in the Center's promo materials.

The sound of music floated through the door, disrupting Sonia's thoughts. She looked up. "Who are those singing?"

Marit smiled. "They're good, aren't they? That's the youth choir. It's their rehearsal day."

Sonia cocked her head. The song was unfamiliar, but the singing was more than decent. Closing her notebook, she turned to Marit. "Thank you so much for your time. Would you object to being part of any publicity

materials I might make for the Center? It wouldn't be intrusive at all—just pictures of you and Haakon and maybe a small interview about why you love coming to the Arts Center?"

"I'd love to do anything I can to help," Marit said.

"Great! I'll send you release forms for your signed consent once everything's decided."

"Thank you, and good luck," Marit said.

Sonia gathered her things and nodded her goodbyes to the other parents in the room. Stepping into the hallway, she followed the sound of singing. It came from the auditorium.

Sonia pushed the heavy doors open and walked into the back of the large hall. On the stage at the front, a group of about thirty teenagers stood in two lines, singing in three-part harmony. As she listened, the chorus stopped, and a young lady began a solo. Goosebumps tickled Sonia's arms. The choir hummed under the melody, joining in as the chorus started again and swelling to a full-throated crescendo.

Sonia's heart thudded. These teens were more than good. With a sound like that, they could be exactly what she needed for her fund-raising plan.

Chapter Eight

AXEL WAS A FEW minutes early to pick up Karla from her pottery class at the Arts Center. While loitering in the hallway, he peered into the room through a glass pane above the door. Karla sat in front of a pottery wheel. Leaning forward with the tip of her tongue poking out of her mouth, her gaze was fixed on the pot that took shape under her clay-covered fingers.

The instructor stood next to Karla, watching the girl work. Karla removed her hands and looked up at the elderly lady, grinning from ear to ear.

Axel's own face stretched with a smile.

He glanced at his watch. The class would continue for ten more minutes. Sonia's office was down the hall. He could use the time to check on whether she had come up with any new fund-raising ideas. But she'd only been working here for a week. In her place, he'd hate to have his boss buzzing around and micromanaging him before he'd settled in.

He pulled his phone out of his pocket. Better to use the time to catch up on his emails. His gut tightened as a new message popped up from the

contractor handling the remodeling work for the Center. That would be the estimates for the roof repair.

Axel opened the email and the attached file, scanning the rows of figures until he reached the grand total of the repair estimate. What was this madness? The repairs were going to cost twice as much as the contractor's original estimate. He focused on each line item. On top of the existing troubles, the contractor had found a dry rot infestation, which needed to be handled immediately. No wonder the bill was so high.

Axel sighed, rubbing the back of his neck. The Center was already operating at a loss. A "white elephant," his financial manager had said. Axel could liquidate some of his own stock to pay for the work, but that was the last resort. A year ago, he wouldn't have minded. But now he had a daughter to think of. His investments were meant to support Karla's future and buying this building had already depleted his funds significantly.

"Oh, there you are."

Axel looked up. His gaze collided with Sonia as she strode toward him on her high heels, gliding down the dingy hallway as though it were a runway in Paris Fashion Week.

She stood in front of him, her face glowing. "I was hoping to see you today. I've had the most amazing idea for a fund-raising showpiece."

He stuffed his phone into his jacket pocket. "Well, I've had the most alarming quote for building repairs. I'm all ears."

"Repairs for the Center?"

"Yes. The contractor found dry rot while inspecting the roof."

She frowned. "That's bad. Can it be fixed?"

"Yes, but it won't be cheap. It needs to be sorted out immediately, and there's no money to do it. So, let's hear about your idea."

Her face brightened. "Okay. It's something that might actually help us raise funds quickly. Why didn't anyone tell me how amazing the youth choir is?"

"Are they? I don't think I've ever heard them."

"You should. They're really good." Her smile broadened. "So good that I think we could build an entire fund-raising campaign around them. There's enough in-house talent to do a musical play. People love live theater shows, especially musicals, and there are so many ways we could leverage that. We could sell tickets and raise money, and we could also get local businessmen to sponsor the show and to underwrite other expenses." As she spoke, she gestured with her hands. "And along with the musical, we could incorporate things that show the

other work the Center is doing. Like artwork made by the clients or costumes made by people from the dressmaking group. We could link it with a gallery exhibition to get people to bid on pieces of art."

"I think that's a wonderful idea." The voice came from behind Axel.

He turned around. He hadn't heard Karla coming through the door. Her eyes were on Sonia.

"Seriously," Karla said. "We should totally do it."

Sonia grinned at Karla. "I'm glad you think so. It could be amazing, especially if everyone gets involved. Do you think the other teens would be interested?"

"Oh, yeah. You'd have no trouble getting volunteers."

Sonia turned to Axel. "What do you think?"

"What sort of timeline do you have in mind?" The repair work could not wait. But putting together a musical took time as well.

"That's the thing. The choir has been working on material that would be suitable. Maybe two months?"

Axel crossed his arms. "That seems tight. Are you sure?"

"I think they could do it if everyone pulls together."

"Okay," Axel said. It wasn't as though other ideas were leaping out at them. "Send me a proposal, including timelines and costs, and we'll talk about it."

Sonia raised her hand in a mock salute. "Aye, aye, captain. You'll have it tomorrow. Talk to you soon." She turned to Karla. "Bye!"

Axel watched Sonia walk down the hallway.

"She's really pretty," Karla said.

He dragged his gaze away from Sonia. "Are you ready? Let's go home."

Chapter Nine

SONIA SAT IN THE fifth row of the auditorium in the Berghaven Community Arts Center, her sore head defying the aspirin she'd taken an hour ago. Her headache throbbed in time with the song the teenage band was murdering as they worked on the instrumental backup for the musical play.

When she'd first heard the youth choir, she'd made the dangerous assumption that, because the vocalists

were so good, the band would also be skilled. Not so.

After three hours of rehearsal, the would-be musicians sounded worse than when they had started this extra practice session at eight this evening. Sonia massaged her temples as, for the twelfth time at least, the band launched into *Freedom's Song*, the show-stopping anthem which gave the musical its name.

The drummer, a long-haired youth, assaulted the song as though it was his only shot at musical stardom, his clumsy beats clobbering the other instruments into the background. Despite the deafening drums, the bass guitarist still had trouble sticking to the tempo. The guitarist stopped playing a few bars into the song. His sight-reading skills were rudimentary at best. All evening long, he'd been losing his place and failing to keep up.

The keyboard player, who also accompanied the choir, was the only competent musician among the lot. He patiently coached his colleagues, but it was no good. It was now well after eleven. But instead of improving, with each repeated playthrough the band found fresh ways to compound their cacophony.

Sonia squeezed her eyes shut as *Freedom's Song* lurched to a stop like a train wreck, with a cymbal clash that left her ears ringing. If things continued this way, the musical showcase would end up being a

platform for humiliation. Her name would be linked to this backwater village disaster and Sonia could forget about rebuilding her reputation as a skilled PR manager.

Nils, the pianist, shoved his glasses farther up his nose and spoke to the other musicians. “Shall we try once more from the top? Maybe take it slower while we figure out the intro. And, Arne, hold back a bit in the opening verse. If you start off with all that energy, you have nowhere else to go by the song’s climax.”

Sonia raised her hand. “No, guys. I think we’d better call it a night. Why don’t you pack your things up?”

The guitarist lifted the strap off his shoulder and Arne stood up from behind his drum kit. As the teens disconnected their instruments from the sound system, Sonia beckoned to Nils. He came to where she stood, and they walked several rows toward the back of the auditorium.

Sonia crossed her arms. "Nils, I have to be honest. I hate to say it, but it's sounding worse than ever before. I'm very concerned."

Nils sighed. "No, we're not sounding great. The music is a bit more complicated than anything the guys have tried, especially Billy. But I think with a bit more time they'll be able to catch up. Or maybe I could simplify their parts and add some extra practice sessions. They're not afraid to work hard."

"The problem is we're running out of time. We only have a few weeks to get this perfect. I have to make a hard decision." Sonia looked at the band as they carefully packed away the expensive sound equipment. They were good kids, always turning up to rehearsals on time.

Sighing, she faced Nils. "This isn't working, so we'll have to move on to Plan B. I found a pre-recorded backing track for the musical. We can use that instead of a live band, and the choir and the soloists will sing along."

Nils blinked at her. "What? But they've been looking forward to playing. I'm sure if we worked a bit more, we could iron things out."

"The decision is made. We don't have any choice," Sonia said. "I'll let them know."

Nils frowned as Sonia walked toward the stage. "Hey, guys. When you're done packing up, please come down here. I'd like to have a word with you."

The band members climbed down the stairs and joined Sonia and Nils.

Sonia forced enthusiasm into her voice. "First of all, thank you for the work you've put in. You volunteered to take part in the musical, and you've shown up for all these hours of extra practice without complaining. I really

appreciate it." She sighed. "That's why it was so hard to make this decision. But time is running out and we're not quite where we need to be with the music. You guys have given it everything you can, but I think we'd better hit the pause button. Maybe you can be a part of the next musical we put on. But for this one, I've decided we will use a pre-recorded backing track."

Arne's face clouded. He shot a glance at Nils, whose gaze was fixed on the floor. "You're replacing us with a backing track?"

"Yes," Sonia said. "Again, I know you've done your best, but it's just a matter of the limited time we have."

"So, all this extra rehearsal was for nothing?" the guitarist asked.

"Absolutely not," Sonia said. "I'm sure it's helped you improve your skills, and in that sense, the work you've put in isn't wasted. And I have lots of other ways you can help with this production. We'll need people to help distribute flyers, to set up props, and do a hundred and one other little things. You'll still be very valuable members of the team and support the fund-raising effort."

"Yeah, whatever." Glaring at Sonia, Arne shouldered the strap of his backpack. "Come on, guys. Let's go."

They strolled out of the hall, none of them looking back at Sonia.

Chapter Ten

AXEL PARKED HIS CAR in its allocated space in front of the Arts Center and bounded up the stairs to the front doors. The afternoons when he checked in here were fast becoming his favorite time of day. He hadn't expected to have much of a hands-on role, but with his finances so tied up with the Center, it made sense to monitor what was going on.

He enjoyed working alone in his home office, managing his developer team remotely. But the buzz and energy in the bustling Arts Center made a pleasant change from solitude at the end of his workday. And the changes were rolling in thick and fast, thanks to Sonia. The woman embodied the force of ten dynamos.

Her office door was closed, a pink Post-it note scribbled with black marker stuck at eye level.

In the auditorium, watching rehearsals. Sonia.

He followed the sound of the music down the hallway.

On the auditorium stage, a group of dancers went through their routine to the rhythm of a catchy instrumental piece.

Sonia stood a few rows from the front, her back toward Axel. Cupping her hands around her mouth, she called to the dancers, "Make sure you use the whole stage. Don't all bunch together in one corner."

As the dancers spread out, she raised both thumbs up. "Much better! Looking good."

Axel stepped forward.

She turned around and saw him. "Oh, hello. Good to see you. Things are shaping up nicely, don't you think?" She gestured toward the stage where the dancers wove in and out of an intricate routine.

"I'm impressed. And by the sound of it, the band has improved a lot as well. They must have been working really hard."

"That's not the band."

Axel looked at her. "It's not?"

"No. The band wasn't working out like we'd hoped. That music is from a pre-recorded backing track."

"Okay," Axel said. "So, are they rehearsing separately until they're ready to join the production?"

Sonia shook her head. "No, we're sticking with the backing track. I gave them as much time as I could, but they just couldn't play well enough. Even with hours of extra rehearsals, they weren't getting any better." Stepping forward, she lowered her voice. "To be

honest, they were a disaster. So, I made the call to go this route."

Something about this didn't sit well with Axel. "How do they feel about being dropped? They gave up a lot of their spare time to work on the musical."

"I know. It wasn't an easy decision to make, and in any other situation I'd have let them persevere. But so much is hinging on this show working out." Her brown eyes held his gaze. "We need to raise funds quickly for the roof repairs and to deal with the dry rot, and this is our best opportunity to do that. If this event is going to draw the kind of sponsors and level of funding we need, the show has to be excellent."

"I thought it was a big selling point to use home-grown talent in this production so we can showcase what the Center does."

She crossed her arms. "We are using home-grown talent, mostly. The dancers, the choir, the soloists, and the entire production crew are regulars at the Arts Center. But being home grown isn't enough. The talent also has to be good."

"I hear what you're saying, but I'm just not sure. How did they take it?"

"Like I said, it wasn't an easy decision, and they were disappointed. But I found ways of including them so they can still help with the fund-raising efforts even if they're not going to be part of the musical. I asked them to distribute promotional flyers. In fact, right now, they should be out distributing those."

Axel pointed to a trash can a few feet away. It was overflowing with paper waste. He stepped over and picked up a piece of paper. "You mean these flyers?"

Sonia's eyes widened as she took in the stacks of flyers that had been dumped in the trash can.

"I don't know what those are doing there, but there must be some mistake." She straightened her shoulders. "Anyway, the rehearsals are coming along very well. This is going to be fantastic."

Still looking at the trash can, Axel prayed she was right. Because, clearly, the band members were not quite as on-board with helping out as she thought.

Chapter Eleven

SONIA GLANCED AT THE clock in the corner of her computer screen. She had forty minutes to submit the Arts Center's application for a charitable grant. Working so close to the deadline wasn't ideal, but until a few weeks ago, she'd not known she would ever need to keep track of submission deadlines for non-profit grant applications.

But she was almost ready. All she had left to do was write the perfect cover letter to send with the other supporting documents. Glancing over the paragraphs she'd already drafted, she screwed up her face. Too impersonal. The cover letter had to tell the Arts Center's story and show these dispensers of charity funds why Berghaven deserved the money. She tapped the delete key, wiping out the lines of text. Thirty-eight minutes to get this right.

A tap sounded on her door. Oh, great. The last thing she needed was an interruption right now. She ought to get a "do not disturb" sign for her door.

She squashed down a sigh. Hopefully, she could quickly get rid of whoever it was. "Come in."

The door opened and Axel's daughter, Karla, took a hesitant step in. Her dark hair was pulled back in a messy bun and she wore the typical teenage uniform of skinny jeans, heavy boots, and a chunky sweater. She clutched a notebook to her chest. "I'm sorry to bother you. Do you have a couple of minutes?"

The word "no" tingled on the tip of Sonia's tongue. She had no time to spare. None. But as she scanned the girl's wide-eyed face, Sonia couldn't make herself tell Karla she was too busy to listen. "Sure. What's on your mind?"

Karla walked forward, holding her notebook in front of her. It resembled an artist's sketchbook, with a ton of other papers and fabric swatches sticking out from between the pages.

"At the rehearsal the other day, you said you had to organize costumes for the musical. I have a few ideas for what the different characters might wear, and I made some mockups and a mood board. I thought maybe you might be interested."

Sonia was indeed interested. The styling and costumes for *Freedom's Song* were among a thousand details that needed attention. She'd delegated responsibility to one of the Center's employees, who hadn't been too keen on the extra work. "Really? Let's have a look. Please sit down."

Karla slid the book over, flipping past a couple of pages. “Here’s my concept for Martha, and on the next page I have some ideas for what John could wear.”

Sonia sucked in a breath. The sketches were amazing. Karla showed a gift for capturing the mood and the personality of the characters. “I love these! You’ve got Martha in loose-flowing pastel-colored outfits. Is that because she’s such a gentle, sensitive person?”

Karla’s face brightened. “That’s what I wanted to get across. And John is solid and dour, so he’s in somber colors.” She turned some more pages over. “I styled looks for each of the three acts. I know we’re on a limited budget, so I only thought of basic pieces you can get at discount clothes chains. We could easily run up the scarves for the dancers on a sewing machine with a bit of cheap fabric. I also researched some prices and have a budget estimate of what it would cost to make all these costumes."

Sonia realized her mouth was hanging open as she stared at the girl. "I'm more than impressed with your initiative in doing this and how incredibly talented you are."

The girl glowed under Sonia's praise; her blue eyes luminescent as she smiled. She had her father's eyes. Sonia had never noticed before.

She spread out her hands. "You know what? I'm happy to let you take the lead on this. Mrs. Hanson was in charge of figuring out the costumes, but she has a lot on her plate. By the look of all you've done, you could do a terrific job. Where did you learn to draw like this? You have an incredible eye for fashion."

"Thank you," Karla said. "My mother was artistic, and she loved nice clothes, especially things that reminded her of old school Hollywood glamor. We'd spend hours sketching together and coming up with different looks. I always made my choices thinking, 'Would Grace Kelly or Audrey Hepburn wear this?' Then we'd go to the mall with just a couple of hundred kroner and see if we could create the looks we had in our mind."

"Your father must be very proud of you."

Karla shrugged. "I don't think he's interested in this type of thing. He's not into fashion. I gave him a really nice beanie and a hoodie for Christmas, but he never wears them." She looked at her hands. "I wish I had my mother's notebooks. We had so many ideas and fabric swatches in there, and some of them might have been useful."

Sonia and Karla turned at the sound of rapping on the door, which stood ajar.

Axel walked in, eyebrows raised as he glanced at Karla. "Here you are. Are you ready to go?"

Karla stood, closing her notebook and dragging it toward herself. "I'll get the rest of my things."

"I'm parked outside. Meet me at the car in five minutes."

Karla glanced at Sonia. "Thank you."

"No, thank *you*. We'll have to talk again soon."

Axel turned a quizzical look toward Sonia as Karla left the office. "What was that about?"

"Your daughter has some serious talent."

"You mean her art? She is pretty good."

"She's more than good. She's amazing," Sonia said. "And not just at fine art. She's got quite an eye for fashion. She was showing me her ideas, and I'm going to let her take the lead on costume design and styling for this production."

Axel rubbed his chin. "I know she loves clothes and hanging out at the mall. But doesn't every teenager? I didn't know she had any special talent for that."

"Oh, she does. She could pursue a career in this if she wanted to. She said she doesn't have her mother's notebooks, which she misses."

Axel shifted his feet. "She said that?"

"Yes. Any idea where they might be?"

"Not really. But I'll look into it."

"You should," Sonia said. "Speaking from experience, I wish I'd kept more of my mother's things when she passed. I would have liked that sense of connection, especially as I got older."

Axel's gaze shifted away from Sonia's. "I said I'd look into it. I'd better get going. We'll catch up tomorrow on the progress of the fund-raising."

Oops. She hoped she hadn't offended him by lecturing about how to parent.

She glanced at the clock. Only twenty minutes left until the deadline. Time to write like the wind. "I'm sending in a grant application right now, and there's another I'll put together next week. And tomorrow I've got a meeting with the Berghaven Chamber of Commerce. I'll let you know how it all goes."

Axel nodded. "Good. See you soon."

He walked out the door as Sonia turned back to her screen. The interruption had cost her precious time. But she was glad she'd given Karla a few minutes.

Chapter Twelve

SONIA'S GRIP TIGHTENED ON her computer mouse. The email from her financial adviser confirmed what she'd been dreading. She wasn't going to recover any of the money she'd invested in Lauritz's company. Her nest egg was cracked, scrambled, and incinerated.

She'd found a buyer for her condo in Trondheim, but after paying off the mortgage and equity loans, she'd be lucky to have anything left over. She let go of the mouse and stretched her cramped fingers. In her mid-forties, she was back to square one and would have to rebuild not just her career but her retirement fund.

She sighed. At least the fund-raising campaign for the Arts Center was going well. If she succeeded with this project, it might lead to better and more lucrative jobs. The articles and updates she'd posted on LinkedIn and on her professional blog were getting some traction and raising her profile.

Someone knocked on her door and Sonia looked up. Axel? What was he doing here? She glanced at her watch. It was well before their agreed check in time.

He came into the office, looking ill-at-ease. "I'm sorry to drop in unannounced. But I could use some help."

"Of course. What can I do?"

He threaded his fingers through his hair. "It's Karla's birthday on Saturday. I ordered her gift weeks ago, but the supplier says they're having delivery chain problems and it won't arrive until after her birthday. So, I need to get something else fast. It'll have to be something I can buy here in Berghaven because there's no time to get anything shipped."

"Okay," Sonia said slowly. Where was he heading with this?

“I hate to impose because this isn’t related to your job, and please feel free to say no. Karla admires your taste. I hoped you would help me choose a gift for her. You’re more likely to know what she would like than I am.”

A rush of warmth bloomed in Sonia’s chest. “I’d be delighted to help, and I’m flattered that she likes my taste. She’s a very artistic and stylish young lady.”

“I know. That’s why I am afraid if I were left to my own devices, I might choose something she’ll hate.” He laughed, but Sonia sensed there was more behind it.

"You said her birthday is on Saturday. When do you want me to get the gift to you?"

He scrunched his face in a sheepish expression. "I was hoping you could come with me to look for it now. Unless you're busy, of course."

"I'm always busy," Sonia said, laughing. "But I can put off work for a couple of hours." A spot of retail therapy was a pleasurable distraction from the gloomy email she'd just got. Even though she wasn't shopping for herself, it would be fun to figure out what Karla might like.

Axel blew out a puff of air. "Thank you. You're a lifesaver."

"Don't thank me yet." Sonia clicked the shutdown button on her computer. "I take shopping seriously, so I hope you're ready to wear out some shoe leather looking for the perfect gift."

Ten minutes later, they stood in a clothes boutique in Berghaven's mall. Axel had said budget wasn't an issue, so Sonia headed straight for whatever caught her eye, without looking at the price tag. Lucky Karla.

Turning to Axel, Sonia fingered a bracelet which came with matching earrings. "When Karla showed me her mood board for the musical's costume design, she mentioned she loves the old, classical Hollywood glamor icons

like Grace Kelly and Audrey Hepburn."

Axel spread out his hands. "What you just said makes no sense to me, but I'm sure it's all true."

"Wait a minute. Her birthday is in May, so her birthstone would be an emerald." Sonia rotated the jewelry display. Good thing Axel hadn't set a budget limit.

She scanned the bracelets for a minute. "What did you give her for Christmas?"

"A chain store gift card and some cash. I couldn't think what else to get." He paused for a beat, then said, "I met her for the first time not long after her thirteenth birthday last year."

The bracelet slipped from Sonia's grasp and she busied herself picking it up and setting it back on the display rack. Axel was losing ground fast. What kind of guy met his daughter for the first time when she was a teenager?

"I didn't know I had a daughter until her mother died."

Heat crept up Sonia's neck. Her judgmental thoughts must have been written all over her face, clear and legible enough for Axel to read them. Time to pivot to a new subject. "What's the other gift you've ordered? The one that's been delayed?"

"A drawing tablet for her designs and other artwork."

"I'm sure she'll love that."

"I hope so."

A purple scarf caught Sonia's eye. "A clever girl like Karla could find a million ways to accessorize with this. What do you think?"

"I defer to your superior judgment."

She winced at his use of the word "judgment." "I think you're doing a decent job. Losing a mother at that age is tough." Sonia knew what it was like to be a motherless teen. Being rudderless on a too-big, storm-tossed ocean with your anchor ripped away. Karla was lucky to have a father to take her in.

A tinge of pink touched Axel's face. Sonia decided that she liked his smile, especially when he was self-conscious. He rifled through the rack of scarves while Sonia studied some leather purses.

Axel cleared his throat. "By the way, I asked my lawyer about getting those notebooks Karla was asking about. He located them and will send them over."

His face was angled away from hers, his gaze fixed on a silk scarf.

"That's great," she said. He'd acted on her unsolicited piece of advice? And here she was, thinking she'd offended him by meddling. "I'm sure Karla will appreciate that."

She wished she'd kept more of her mother's things. Not that there was much for her to hold on to. Most of their property had been threadbare junk only fit for the town dump, and in her burning desire to escape Berghaven, she'd not taken anything with her.

"So, why did you move away from Berghaven?" he asked.

She gaped at him. Did this guy have mind-reading powers? "Do you want the truth or the sanitized press release?"

"The truth, please," he said, smiling.

"Okay." She drew in a deep breath. "The truth, but only the concise version. I was dirt poor and sick of being treated like a charity case who needed to survive on handouts. So I moved to the city to make my fortune."

She didn't know what she expected to see in his face. Shock, perhaps? Pity? Or embarrassment followed by a swift change of subject? His blue eyes softened. "It's hard to reinvent yourself in a small town. But it seems you managed to do that."

"Oh, yeah. I did it so well that I'm back here all over again." She meant to keep her tone light, but an edge crept through.

"Berghaven isn't all bad, is it?" Axel asked.

"It has its positives if you don't mind living in a place where everyone knows everyone else's business." She moved away from the purses, returning to the jewelry display. "How about you? What brought you here?"

He grinned. "I wanted the obscurity."

She tapped her chin, frowning in mock thoughtfulness. "Well, maybe don't go buying community arts centers if you want to be an obscure citizen."

She liked his laugh as much as his smile.

Chapter Thirteen

AXEL LIFTED THE LID of the waffle iron, revealing a perfect golden brown waffle. He slid it on top of a freshly made stack and put the plate in the middle of the table.

He'd used the good china, setting out raspberry and blueberry jam and sour cream along with those little spoons his grandmother loved so much.

A small pile of wrapped presents—the ones Sonia picked out—sat next to

Karla's plate. The drawing tablet he'd ordered as Karla's main gift was still delayed, making him even more grateful for Sonia's help choosing these stand-in presents.

He walked to the hallway and called out, "Breakfast is ready."

Karla emerged from her room, stopping short when her gaze fell on the table. "Wow, you've made an effort. We're eating in the dining room?"

"It's your birthday, so I thought we'd eat here for once instead of in the kitchen."

She looked up at him, her smile burrowing deep into his heart. "Thanks."

"Would you like to eat first, or open your presents? One of them won't get here until next week, but I hope you like these."

Karla sat down, touching a large package. "Presents first." She ripped off the shiny wrapping paper, beaming as she pulled out a pink and gray canvas backpack with a matching cross body tote bag and coin purse. "I love them!"

Axel searched her face, letting out a breath slowly at her genuine delight. Thank God Sonia had been there to help him choose the gifts. He wouldn't have had a clue otherwise. Karla was already opening the second package, also one of Sonia's picks.

She held up a delicate white gold neck chain with an emerald pendant. "This is amazing, Dad. How did you know I wanted this?"

Axel froze. Did she realize she'd just said "Dad?" The word socked him like a sucker punch to the gut. She stared at him, waiting for an answer.

He cleared his throat. "So, you like it?"

"Like it? I absolutely love it!" She fiddled with the clasp and fastened the chain around her neck. "How does it look?"

"Perfect."

He'd been a father for fourteen years, but never been called "Dad" until today. A bitter aftertaste stained the sweet warmth that came with the word. Annika had robbed him of years of fatherhood, of the chance to see his daughter growing up.

His mind strayed to the box with Annika's things that sat tucked away in the closet. It had arrived from his lawyer a couple of days ago. Convinced by Sonia's suggestion to help his daughter stay connected with her mother, he'd planned to give it to Karla today. And then she'd said "Dad." He'd missed so many of her birthdays. Couldn't he hoard one for himself without sharing it with Annika's lingering presence?

Karla unwrapped the last gift, an artist's set with drawing pens,

graphite pencils, and a kneaded eraser inside a carrying case. "This is awesome! And look, it fits in my new backpack."

Axel grinned back. "You're welcome. Come on, let's eat before the waffles get cold."

He stood and grabbed the discarded wrapping paper and ribbons while Karla helped herself to a couple of waffles. Placing the paper in the bin, he glanced up at his daughter. *Dad*. The sketchbooks and mementos in the box were all she had left of her mother. He wouldn't be like Annika. Karla needed both her parents.

Drawing in a slow breath, he walked past the dining room and into his study. He opened the closet and stared at the corrugated cardboard box. The day it had come, he'd only glanced inside once, and he didn't know what it contained, beyond his lawyer's words that he'd sent Annika's sketchbooks and scrapbooks. He dragged the box out and took it into the dining room. "I have one more thing for you."

She looked up, her gaze immediately locking onto the box. "What's that?"

"My solicitor sent this over. It contains some things that belonged to your mother. They're yours now." He set the box on the dining table.

Karla stood up slowly, pushing her chair back. She lifted the lid and peered inside, the color leaching from her face. She slammed the lid back on and picked up the box, her face straining with effort.

"That thing is heavy. Do you want some help?"

"No."

He watched her struggle down the hallway, lugging the box into her room. A dull thud told him she'd put it on the ground, then her door closed.

His gaze shifted to the breakfast table. Karla's half-eaten waffles sat there, next to her gifts. Things had been going so well. Had he just blundered by giving her that box?

He sat at the table, but a hard knot in his stomach robbed him of all desire to eat. He bowed his head and prayed. *Lord, please cover Karla. Lead her thoughts to healthy places. Protect her heart from depression, bitterness, and anger.*

He glanced at Karla's still-closed bedroom door. What was she doing? What was going through her head? He went up to the door and knocked gently. "Karla, I wanted to get tickets to *The Prince's Oath* in Havdal. There's an afternoon showing and if we leave now, we'd have time to window shop and grab lunch first."

Her reply, when it eventually came, was muffled, as though she were

talking into her pillow. "I don't want to see it."

The knot in his stomach solidified into dread. Karla loved movies. She was turning down a chance to go see one in the theater?

He walked back to the dining room and picked up his unused plate and cutlery. Praying with every step, he cleared away the jam and sour cream and wrapped the waffles and Karla's plate in plastic wrap. There was still no sound from her room.

Grabbing the TV remote, he sat on the edge of the sofa. The channels clicked past in a meaningless blur before he settled on a soccer match. Rosenborg was playing Sandefjord.

Men bounded up and down the field chasing a little ball and commentators gushed about it as though it mattered. And while this pointless spectacle played out, his daughter was hurting, and he was powerless to help. He stared at the screen as the minutes ticked by.

A roar from the crowd on TV signaled the match was over. He glanced at the clock on the screen. How was it already lunchtime?

He went to Karla's bedroom door and knocked. "Karla? Do you want something to eat?"

"No."

"Are you sure? You hardly touched your breakfast."

"I said no, okay?"

He stood outside her door, ransacking his brain for something to say or do.

She spoke again. "And stop hovering."

His phone rang as he headed back to the living room. He glanced at the caller ID. Sonia. "Hello."

"Hi, Axel. Did you forget about our meeting?"

Axel frowned. "What meeting?"

"The meeting that was supposed to have started fifteen minutes ago. You were going to sign off on my proposal package so I can courier a new grant application. Remember?"

“Oh, right. Sorry. I... It completely slipped my mind.” Sonia needed his signature so urgently that he’d agreed to have this meeting not just on a Saturday, but on his daughter’s birthday. But concern about Karla had driven it completely out of his head.

“Axel, are you okay?”

Ninety-nine times out of a hundred, Axel would have brushed off the question with a terse, “I’m fine.” Instead, he blurted out, “I gave Karla the box with her mother’s things. She’s shut herself in her room all morning and is refusing to come out.”

“Aw, poor kid. I’m so sorry to hear that. Grief comes in unpredictable waves. You’re doing okay one moment

and then, wham, it slams into you with no warning, and you just want to crawl into a dark hole and cry all day. And you said it's her first birthday without her mother, right?"

Axel nodded. "That's right. Maybe I shouldn't have given her that box today. It might have been too much when it's already a big milestone day."

"You couldn't have known for sure how she'd take it. I had a huge random meltdown once when I smelled a spicy curry. It was something completely normal, but it triggered a memory of a meal I had with my mother. But things like this are all part of the process. Don't blame yourself, okay?"

"Thanks." Her words were encouraging, but Axel wasn't convinced. He ought to have held off a couple of days before giving Karla her mother's things.

"Listen," Sonia said, "I don't want to put pressure on you when you've already got a situation, but I need you to sign off on these documents. Could I quickly bring them over?"

"Yes, that would be best. I don't want to leave her alone."

"I'm on my way."

Chapter Fourteen

SONIA STOOD AT THE doorstep of Axel's house, her arms loaded with carrier bags of Chinese takeaway and a large document folder. She maneuvered her baggage so she could just about hit the doorbell with an elbow, but hesitated before pushing the button.

Bringing food had been a spur-of-the-moment idea. Now, though, she felt silly and presumptuous. Axel had a family situation going on, one which had resulted from her own ill-timed advice.

She half turned to face her car. She could be gone with just a few steps. But what about the documents Axel needed to sign? Without his immediate sign-off, she wouldn't be able to courier her proposal on time, and that might cost them some crucial funding. She'd just knock on the door, have him sign the papers, and leave.

She shifted her stance, causing the aromatic scent of the takeaway food to waft up to her nose. *Bother.* She should put the food back in her car, then come back and get Axel to sign the papers.

She took a step toward her car, but froze when the front door opened.

Axel peered out, his features relaxing when he saw Sonia. "I thought I heard a car pulling up. Thanks for stopping by with the documents." His gaze landed on the carrier bags. "Something smells good."

Ah, well. No escaping now. Sonia held the bags out. "I grabbed this from the Golden Dragon in case you haven't had a chance to cook anything with all that's been going on today."

Axel took the bags, a smile breaking out on his face. "Thanks. You really didn't have to, but I'm grateful. Karla loves Chinese food, and I'm quite partial to it myself. Come in."

Sonia followed him into the house, turning her head to look around. It looked just like him–fuss-free, minimalist design with no clutter anywhere. Marie Kondo would approve.

He led the way into his kitchen, where stainless steel gleamed alongside granite surfaces. Axel set the bag of food on a countertop and pointed to the kitchen island. "If you can get out the things you want me to look at, I'll dish up the food."

Sonia pulled out the documents, scanning through them and setting in order the pages that needed his signature. She glanced up as Axel brought plates to the kitchen table. He was setting three places.

He looked at her. "I assume you'll stay to eat?"

Warmth crept up her neck and into her face. She hadn't thought that far. Her impulse had just been to get him and Karla some food. Now it hit her that he might think she was inviting herself for a meal. "I only ordered food for you and Karla."

"Come on." He gestured at the open cartons. "There's plenty here. Much more than Karla and I could handle."

Protesting would probably be more awkward than giving in. "Okay. Thank you." She turned away and busied herself with the documents again, not caring to examine the thrill that passed through her body at the thought of sharing a meal with him.

He came over to the papers she'd laid out and scribbled his signature. "There you go. I'll tell Karla to come and eat."

Axel headed down the hallway and Sonia's gaze strayed after him. A minute later, he came back, his face clouded. "She says she's not hungry, but she's not had anything since breakfast. She hardly touched even that."

Axel stood next to the table, staring at a white carton. Seconds ticked by, and his stillness unnerved Sonia.

He burst into sudden movement, grabbing a plate and scooping out a portion of egg-fried rice. "I'll leave this outside her door. She's got to eat something." He added cashew chicken and vegetables and picked up a knife and fork.

He went back along the hallway.

Sonia eyed the front door. Major family stuff was happening here, and she didn't need to get entangled in it. Now that he'd signed the documents, she'd slip out and leave him to handle his troubles in private.

Axel came back to the kitchen, both hands pushed into his hair. He glanced at Sonia. "I left the plate outside the door so she can eat if she wants to. Thanks for bringing it. Chinese food is the most likely thing to get her to eat. Have a seat."

Studying his face, Sonia lowered herself into a dining chair. "Listen, I understand if you'd rather that I go now. It's not a problem."

He stared at her, frowning. "No, I'm glad you came. I forgot our meeting and put you to the trouble of coming here. And you were thoughtful enough to bring us some food, too. Shall we help ourselves before this gets cold?"

They filled their plates and ate in silence.

The atmosphere became intolerably heavy. She had to address the elephant in the room. "Listen. It was my idea

that you give Karla her mother's sketchbooks, and I kind of badgered you about it. I didn't think it would upset her, and I'm really sorry if it has."

Axel looked up at her, blinking. "What? No, it's not your fault. I thought it was the right thing to do. And, like you said before, none of us could have known how she'd take it. If nothing else, it's shown me that perhaps I need to look into grief counseling. I'm clearly not doing enough for her, and it was obtuse of me not to think of it before."

"You're doing a pretty good job, from what I can see."

His eyes warmed. “Thank you. I appreciate you saying that.”

“It’s true. From where I stand, you’re a decent dad. Trust me as someone who’s been fourteen before. She doesn’t need you to be perfect. She just needs to know you have her back.” Sonia smiled. “And maybe wear one of her gifts every once in a while? I’ve heard about a neglected hoodie and beanie.”

Axel smiled back, and it was good to see the worry lines fade. “Point taken. I’ll wear the hoodie and consider the beanie.” He gestured at the food. “Do you want any more? There’s lots left.”

"No thanks. I'm stuffed." Sonia patted her tummy. "I'll help you clear the table."

Brushing off his protests, she gathered their plates and cutlery while Axel picked up an armload of cartons.

"Where should I put these?" Sonia asked.

Axel pulled a cabinet door open, revealing a dishwasher. "In here. Thank you."

Sonia slotted the plates and cutlery into the dish racks and went back to the table to get the remaining cartons. "Do you want to store the rest of this food somewhere? Chinese takeout is just as delicious the next day."

"Sure. I'll get some containers." He opened another cabinet where plastic food tins stood lined up in precise rows. He'd probably have a heart attack if he got a load of her disorganized cupboards. Wait, she didn't have cupboards anymore. Not since she'd sold her condo.

Sonia put the leftover rice, noodles, and stir-fried beef into the containers Axel had put on the countertop.

"I was wondering about something. You said Karla's only been in your life since last year. How did that happen?" Sonia immediately thought better of her question and added, "Not to pry, of course. You don't need to tell me anything."

Axel paused, dishcloth in hand. “I don’t mind you asking.” He closed his eyes for a moment and sighed. “Karla’s mother was my first proper girlfriend. It may surprise you to know that I was a very shy and awkward young man.”

He smiled, and Sonia chuckled. “Really? That’s shocking!”

“I know, right? But both of us were immature. Looking back, I’d say it was more than that. We were toxic together and brought out the worst in each other. I was jealous and clingy, and Annika seemed to enjoy pushing my buttons. Both of us drank too much, and that never helps. Sometimes I wish I could go back in time and punch myself in the head for being such an idiot.”

Axel's smile was gone now. "And then she got pregnant. After the shock wore off, I was looking forward to being a father. I wanted us to get married and probably got too pushy and territorial with her. We had a huge fight, and she dumped me. She told me the baby wasn't mine and left before Karla was born."

Axel stared at his hands for such a long moment that Sonia wondered if he'd forgotten she was there. He spoke again. "I was a mess. It was as though the bottom had fallen out of my world and I was just spiraling. If I hadn't met someone who invited me to his church, I'd probably not be here today. Anyway, I got the help I needed. Some of it, anyway. And I

didn't hear from Annika again until last year. Her lawyer contacted me to tell me she was terminally ill, and that Karla was, in fact, my daughter. Annika wanted me to take custody of her."

"Wow. That was quite an upheaval. For both of you."

He looked up. "You can say that again. I feel as though I'm groping in the dark most of the time. Like I'm going to mess her up for the rest of her life."

Sonia reached for his hand, her fingers closing over his clenched fist. His hand relaxed and his fingers gripped hers. "Karla's very lucky to have a dad like you."

His eyes glistened, and he blinked quickly.

She squeezed his hand, and a powerful longing to touch his face suddenly hit her. She stepped forward, hand stretched out. Something moved in her peripheral vision.

Axel spun toward the door, dropping Sonia's hand. "Karla. Are you okay?"

Karla stood a few feet away, holding an empty plate, her gaze darting first to Axel and then to Sonia.

15

Chapter Fifteen

SONIA WHIPPED HER HAND back to her side as Axel moved toward his daughter.

"Are you all right, sweetheart?"

Glancing at Sonia, Karla nodded her head.

Axel grabbed Karla's empty plate and fork and set them down next to the sink. "Would you like something to drink?"

"Yes, please." Karla slid onto one of the tall stools at the breakfast bar.

Time to make an exit. Sonia went over to the documents that still sat on the kitchen island. "I'll take these and be on my way. See you later."

Headed toward the fridge, Axel half-turned toward Sonia, his gaze not quite meeting her eyes. His expression was unreadable. "Thanks for stopping by, and thanks for dinner."

Although she'd decided to leave, it stung that he was equally keen for her to go. How else should he be, though? Karla needed his full attention. Sonia nodded at them both and hurried to the front door.

How much had Karla seen? More importantly, what on earth had been going on? Her hand still tingled from contact with Axel's. There was no mistaking the buzz that kicked her pulse into overdrive and caused her stomach to flutter. She had never expected to feel that around Axel, of all people. But there it was. An undeniable attraction.

Sonia got into her car and made the short drive to Lisa's place. Picking up the documents that had seemed so important an hour ago, she let herself into the house. She needed to unpack what had happened and what was going on in her head.

Curled on the sofa with a thick hardback novel, Lisa looked up as

Sonia walked in. “Hi. I was expecting you a bit earlier. I already ate, but your dinner is still warm in the slow cooker.”

Sonia dumped her purse and document folder on the coffee table and sank into an armchair. “Thanks, but I already had dinner. With Axel.”

Lisa sat upright. “You had dinner with Axel? I didn’t know you guys were that close.”

“We’re not. Or, at least, we weren’t. I went to his place with some things that needed signing. We got to talking, and it became kind of deep and intense. I nearly kissed him. I wanted to kiss him.”

Lisa's eyebrows flew skyward. "Get out of here. What?"

"I know, right?" Sonia rubbed the back of her neck.

"I didn't even know you were attracted to him."

"Neither did I."

Lisa leaned forward. "Go on. Spill the details. What was this deep and intense conversation about?"

"You know he's only known about Karla since last year, right?" Sonia tucked her feet under herself. "He told me his ex kept him in the dark about Karla being his, and sprung the news on him when she—Karla's mother, I mean—was about to die. He's worried he's not a good enough dad. Hearing him talk made me see him in a new light. I wanted to make him feel better and I held his hand. Before I knew it, all I could think about was touching his face and kissing him. And then Karla walked in."

"Wow. That's a lot. How did Karla react?"

"She just looked at us. I'm not sure what she saw. I made myself scarce after that, and Axel was so fully focused on Karla that I doubt he even noticed me leave."

Lisa leaned back onto the sofa. "So, what happens now? Are you open to a relationship with him?"

"I don't know." Sonia stood and paced behind the armchair. "The fact that we work together might make it awkward. Plus, he seems pretty tied to Berghaven and I'm not sure I want to stay here long term."

"Aren't you forgetting something? Several things, actually."

Sonia frowned. "What?"

"There's a young girl involved. A very vulnerable young girl who's had a lot of upheaval and needs stability."

"Of course I'm not forgetting Karla. I actually liked her first. Anyway, we're putting the cart before the horse. I already said I'm not sure what I want, and Axel may not even be thinking about dating." She stopped short, gripping the back of the armchair. “He’s not dating, is he?”

Lisa laughed. “No, I’m pretty sure he’s single. Anyway, I’ll pray for you. And you pray about it, too. But guard your heart. You never know. Something wonderful might come out of it. The most important thing is to pray and wait on God to make things clear.”

Sonia’s jaw tightened. Pray. That was the perfunctory advice doled out by rote by all good Christians. She, too, once believed in taking things to God in prayer and trusting in his provision. But prayer hadn’t made a difference when it really counted. She’d prayed, but her mother still died. She’d prayed, but her career still

imploded. God's answers to her prayers had mostly been "no" and a slammed door. If she wanted a relationship with Axel, chances were God would say no to that, too.

"Hey," Lisa said. "I know I sound like a wet blanket for not encouraging you to go full steam ahead. But when you have a failed marriage behind you, you get a bit gun shy."

"It's not that—never mind." Maybe it was best she kept her quarrels with God to herself. Lisa's own unanswered prayers about her estranged husband were another big, fat bone Sonia had to pick with God.

She picked up her document folder. "I'd better get these ready to drop off at the courier's before they close. Thanks for the advice."

"Anytime. I'll pray, and I'm here if you need to talk some more."

Sonia forced a smile and headed for her room.

Chapter Sixteen

A JUMBLE OF CONFLICTING impulses roiled inside Axel as Sonia's footsteps retreated to the front door. Something had sparked between them, a deep resonant chord that hung unresolved at Karla's entrance.

But his disarrayed emotions over Sonia would have to wait. Karla was here now.

Pulling open the fridge, his gaze ranged over the beverages. "What would you like to drink? Juice? Milk?

A soda? We only have cola, but I can go to the corner shop and get you something else."

"Orange juice, please."

He filled a glass and set it on the breakfast bar, where Karla sat examining her short fingernails. What had she seen? Did she walk in while he was holding Sonia's hand? Or when—

"Thanks." She pulled the glass toward herself. "And thanks for the food. I didn't realize how hungry I was."

"Do you want any more? There's plenty left. Or maybe you'd like some dessert? We haven't had your cake yet."

A hint of a smile touched her face, and some of the tension in his shoulders eased. "I'd forgotten about cake. Maybe later."

She sipped her juice and Axel stood irresolute. Would she mind if he joined her at the breakfast bar? But if he plopped himself next to her, it might look like he was pushing her to talk. Hunting for an excuse to linger but not intrude, he grabbed a microfiber cloth from the sink and wiped down the kitchen island.

"Could you tell me who some of the people in those photos are?"

He stared at her. "Which photos?"

"The ones in the box with Mom's things."

Pulse kicking up, he nodded. “Ah, okay. Yes, of course I will. If I know them.” He shot a prayer heavenward while Karla jumped off the stool and went to her room. Playing it cool was the way to go.

She came out of her bedroom holding a dusky pink scrapbook. Perching on her stool, she set the scrapbook on the counter. The album’s cover was decorated with stickers, paper daisies, and ribbon. The words “Karla’s Story” looped across the middle in extravagant hand lettering. This had Annika’s fingerprints all over it. It was exactly the kind of crafty thing she used to love doing.

Karla opened the first page, and Axel stared at a picture of himself from fifteen years ago. His bushy hair, still unmarked by any gray, fell across his forehead, skimming the top of his thick-rimmed Coke-bottle glasses. Underneath the picture, in Annika's flowery script, were the words: ***Axel Vikhammer. Your father.***

His throat tightened. "You said this came with the box?"

"Yes. I've never seen it before. There was also a letter inside, so I think Mom wanted me to have it when she was gone."

So Annika had put this together as a way of introducing Karla to her father. The scrapbook and letter must have gotten lost in the shuffle with all the busyness after Annika's death. If Sonia hadn't prompted him to reach out to his solicitor, who knew how long this might have sat gathering dust?

Karla pointed to a picture on the next page. "It says this is my great-grandmother. But who are they?"

The lump in Axel's throat expanded, making it hard to push his words out. "Yes, that's my grandmother Sigrid and two of her neighbors, Ingunn and Frank Lovseth. Your mother and I often spent Christmas with Sigrid, your great-grandmother. She was the only family I had."

At least, he'd thought she was. Until he learned he had a daughter. *Farmor* would have loved meeting her great-granddaughter. Yet more collateral damage in his and Annika's toxic breakup.

He looked at the date below the photo. This would have been the last Christmas he and Annika had spent as a couple.

In a picture on the next page, Annika smiled coyly at the camera, her hands cradling a visibly pregnant belly. Axel remembered snapping that photo just weeks before their big fight. The one where Annika had told him the baby wasn't his.

"Why did you and Mom split up?"

Karla's voice pulled Axel back into the present, but her question probed an old wound, one he'd often picked at before it finally scabbed over.

Her gaze was fixed on his face. Pure, innocent, piercing into his heart, challenging him to tell the truth and to be open. He wanted to build a connection with her. It looked like the first step would involve him opening up to her and not the other way around.

But how could he answer truthfully without letting his regrets and unresolved anger bubble out of his mouth? He didn't know what Annika had told her. Had she laid all the blame on him?

He weighed each word as though he were picking his way through a minefield. "Your mother and I both made mistakes. I was young, stupid, and very insecure. We loved each other as much as we were able to, but we fought a lot. By the end, your mother wanted nothing to do with me, and I can't say that I blamed her because we were only hurting each other. Not long before you were born, she told me you weren't mine and when she left, I didn't go after her. I think she knew that telling me I wasn't your father was the only way to keep me away. If I'd known that you were mine, I would have been after you like a shot."

"Really?" Her eyes, still locked on his, filled with tears.

"Really. I would never have chosen to miss even a single minute of your life."

Karla leaned into him and he wrapped his arm around her, his vision misting over. For the first time in fourteen years, he was getting to hold his daughter.

Chapter Seventeen

JUGGLING HER TABLET AND coffee-filled travel mug, Sonia sat at the back of the Berghaven Community Arts Center auditorium. She didn't attend rehearsals every day, but with just a couple of weeks until the musical's first public performance, she needed to see for herself how everything was coming along.

Nils the pianist, now elevated to musical director, had told her the entire cast of dancers, actors, soloists, and choir were rehearsing together every day. As the singers belted out the musical's big showpiece, the dancers moved in unison, their choreography smooth and graceful.

Axel should see this. He trespassed on her thoughts more and more since their shared meal on Saturday. She'd glimpsed him and Karla at church yesterday, but there hadn't been time to talk.

Goosebumps prickled on Sonia's skin as the music rose to a crescendo. But something was missing. Birgitta, the lead female vocalist, should have sung a high piercing descant. Instead, the blond girl grimaced and fell silent, her hand flying up to her throat.

Sonia frowned. Was Birgitta unwell? The girl slid back into the song, building up again to the bridge and key change. Instead of the soaring pure note the song called for, her voice cracked. Face flushed, she fell silent again, shaking her head. The music continued, the choir ending the song while the dancers finished their choreography.

As the final chords rang through the auditorium, Sonia got to her feet. Cupping her hands around her mouth, she called out, "Good job, everyone. Let's take a ten-minute break. Birgitta and Nils, would you come here for a minute, please?"

The dancers and choir members scattered from the stage. Sipping from her travel mug, Sonia watched Birgitta and Nils walk to the back of the auditorium. Birgitta's cheeks were still a bright pink and Nils squeezed her shoulder.

Sonia crossed her arms while the pair sat. "That was mostly good. But, Birgitta, you didn't seem very comfortable up there. Is anything the matter?"

Birgitta and Nils exchanged glances, and the girl looked back at Sonia. "It's the first time I've performed the song miked up with the backing track."

Nils chimed in. "The key the song was written in isn't ideal for Birgitta. It's in G Major and changes to A Major. When we sang it with the

band, I had transposed it down to D Major, which suits Birgitta's vocal range. But the backing track is in G Major, like the sheet music. It's five semitones higher than what we were doing, which is a pretty big jump."

Sonia frowned. "Are you saying the song is too high for you?"

"I honestly don't know." Birgitta slumped in her seat. "Sometimes it's okay, but I feel the strain of it, especially when I'm miked up."

Nils said, "Birgitta has an amazing voice, but she shouldn't force herself to sing outside her range, especially when the song is so demanding."

Sonia crossed her arms. "What are we going to do about it? The VIP preview performance is in a couple of weeks."

Birgitta wiped her eyes. Glancing at her, Nils said, "My brother is a sound technician, and he once told me about an app that can digitally transpose a backing track. I can find out more about it, and maybe we could use that."

"You mean transpose the song to a key Birgitta is more comfortable singing?"

Nils nodded. "Yes."

"Would the transposing be necessary for all the other songs Birgitta's doing?"

Nils looked at Birgitta. The girl said, "*Freedom's Song* is the trickiest, but it would be helpful if all the songs could be taken down a few tones."

Sonia liked the sound of this idea less and less. "But then there are other people also singing with you. If the music is transposed, how would it affect them?"

"They were handling the lower key fine before we used the backing track," Birgitta said, her lower lip sticking out.

Sonia rubbed her forehead. This was not the type of snag she wanted to run into two weeks before a sneak peek performance for VIP donors. Using an app to fiddle with the keys sounded too risky when they had limited time with which to get ready.

What if this app didn't work the way it was supposed to? What if it caused additional technical difficulties? She shook her head. "Before we risk tampering with the backing track, I want to try something else. Let's do the song again, with Julie taking the lead vocals."

Birgitta's face paled, then flooded with color.

Sonia stood, waving at Julie, Birgitta's understudy. "Could you try singing Birgitta's part in the song we just did?"

Surprise written all over her face, Julie, a willowy brunette, nodded.

Sonia gestured to the sound guy. "Start the track."

Julie picked up a microphone as the song's opening chords rang out. Her voice, while not as full as Birgitta's, had a pleasing, light tone. The dancers and choir members stood in small groups, staring at Julie.

Sonia tensed as the problem area came, but Julie nailed the high notes without breaking a sweat, even after the climactic key change.

As the song came to an end, Sonia had made up her mind. She might be stepping on people's toes, but experience had taught her it was better to be firm with tough decisions instead of waffling around. Steeling herself, she called the singers and the pianist together.

"This is what we are going to do. Our VIP preview performance is happening in just a couple of weeks. Julie, you'll play Martha."

Birgitta's head jerked up and Nils started to speak, but Sonia held up a hand.

"You've done a great job so far, Birgitta, and your singing is phenomenal. Although your voice is amazing, this key thing is a problem. Two weeks before our first performance, it's too risky to mess around with an app that none of us knows about. I hate to make a last-

minute cast change like this, but we're short on time."

Face turned down, Birgitta muttered, "Okay."

"You're sure you're okay? I wish we could figure out a different solution, but time isn't on our side." She peered at Birgitta's face a few moments longer, but the girl did not meet her gaze. Sonia spoke to the group. "The second thing I have to say is, can everyone who's under eighteen please ensure that you return those signed release forms from your parents or guardians? Julie, I don't have yours yet, and there are a few others. Bring those over ASAP, okay?" She looked around the group, catching a few nods. "Good. Shall we move on to the next scene? Boys, you're up."

As the lead actor and his co-stars assembled on the stage, Sonia walked back to her place at the back of the auditorium.

Nils came up to her, shuffling his weight from foot to foot as he stood in the aisle.

Sonia looked up at him. "Is there something you want to say?"

"Yeah. Um... It's just this thing about Birgitta." Nils sat in the row in front of Sonia, resting his elbows on the back of the seat. "Her grandfather is terminally ill, and the family has been told he probably won't make it through the summer. He was looking forward to seeing her perform in the lead role. Birgitta would never tell you, but I think she's absolutely gutted about not being able to do this for him. Are you sure we can't reconsider this? I think the app will work. I can get my brother to help us out."

Sonia's heart sank like a lead weight. It was hard enough to make tough calls like this without hearing all of this extra backstory. But her priority had to be the Center.

Sighing, she shook her head. "I'm sorry about Birgitta's grandfather. I really am. But we have to think about the whole Arts Center and everyone else who is depending on this musical to be a success. This show could potentially get us solid sponsors so we can keep the doors open, and we just can't risk it going wrong. Do you understand?"

Nils stared at her for a long moment. He turned back to the stage, and Sonia followed his gaze to where Birgitta sat. Nils faced Sonia again, his expression blank. "Yes. I get it."

"What if we do this? Birgitta can perform a solo before the play begins, sort of like an opening act. Her grandfather can still see her sing on the stage. Would that make it up to her?"

Nils shrugged, getting to his feet. "I guess. It's not the same as the lead role, but it's better than nothing."

As he walked away, a whisper of doubt chilled Sonia's thoughts. She pushed it aside. There was no room to entertain indecision. This show had to succeed. She'd tell Birgitta now about being an opening act. Maybe that would console her over losing the lead role.

18

Chapter Eighteen

SONIA KICKED OFF HER pumps and sunk her grateful toes into the emerald green grass of Berghaven Memorial Park. The spring weather, sun-drenched but not too hot, was perfect for a day of photo shoots. Hans,. a talented young photographer, stood nearby, adjusting his tripod. They'd spent the last few hours taking promotional photos of the play's cast members and other key people in the Arts Center. And now it was Axel's turn.

Hans pointed across the field. “There he comes. Bang on time.”

Axel walked toward them, wearing a dark blazer, tan pants, and a white shirt buttoned all the way up to his neck. With his dark hair slicked back, he looked the same as in the dated, unflattering head shots he used on his online platforms. The very pictures Sonia wanted to replace.

Tugging at his shirt collar with a finger, he smiled as he approached them. “I’m ready for my close-up.”

“Let’s get started,” Hans said.

Sonia watched as Hans directed Axel to stand half turned to the camera. Axel stood ramrod straight, chin pointing toward the blue sky.

Hans peered through his camera. “Do you think you could relax a bit?”

Axel rolled his shoulders and positioned himself like a tin soldier, his arms fixed by his side.

Hans clicked a few pictures. “How about a smile?”

Axel bared his teeth, looking more like he was enduring a medical procedure than posing for a portrait.

Sonia walked to where Hans stood as he snapped several more pictures. Axel couldn’t look stiffer if he’d dipped himself in starch. At this rate, they would do better to stick with his old portraits.

"Hang on a minute, Hans," she said. "Axel, you need to relax. How about a joke?"

He glanced at her. "What, you want me to tell you one?"

"I thought I'd tell you one, but go ahead."

"Okay," he said. "Um... what do you call a can opener that doesn't work?"

"What?"

"A can't opener."

Sonia groaned. "That's what I call a dad joke."

Axel grinned. "Well, I *am* a dad. Can you do any better?"

"As a matter of fact, I can. Why can't you trust an atom?"

He screwed up his face. "I give up. Why?"

"Because they make up everything."

He laughed, not a polite social chuckle, but a deep belly laugh that made her feel ridiculously pleased that he found her joke funny. His shoulders relaxed and color rushed to his face.

"These are looking a lot better," Hans said from behind his camera. "Tell him more jokes."

Sonia smiled. "How about a tongue twister? Say this. Which rich witch switched the Swiss wristwatches?"

"Which witch swished the rich witch watches?"

"Nope. Try again."

"Which rich witch switched the Swiss rich watches."

She doubled over with laughter while he made another stab at the tongue twister.

He threw up his hands. "It's impossible."

Wiping the corners of her eyes, Sonia stepped toward Hans. "Let's have a look at what you've got."

Hans swiped through several images on his camera. They were acceptable, but not quite what Sonia wanted. There was something she knew was inside him—a deep vibrant charisma—which wasn't transferring into the images.

She looked up at Axel. "Would you mind taking your jacket off?"

"Okay. It's getting rather warm, anyway."

Sonia walked to him as he laid his blazer on the ground. "And unbutton your shirt sleeves as well. I want to try something. May I?"

Her fingers brushed against the smooth skin of his forearms as she folded back his sleeves. She kept her face angled downward as warmth bloomed into her cheeks. Clearing her throat, she stepped back and appraised Axel in what she hoped was

a professional-looking way. "Loosen your top button."

He obeyed.

"One last thing, if you don't mind." She rummaged in her purse and pulled out a brush. "I've been itching to mess up your hair."

Heat seared her face. Had she actually said that out loud?

With a few deft strokes, she disrupted his slicked back hair, teasing it back into its natural waves.

She stepped back to admire the effect, glad for the excuse to study him.

His eyes searched her face. "Do I look okay?" He didn't ask in the coy, flirty way of a person fishing for a compliment. The genuineness of his question tugged at her heart.

"You look fine." *Really fine.* "I think we're ready, Hans. Try the tongue twister again."

Axel grinned and gave it another go while Sonia went back to join Hans.

A few minutes later, Hans looked up. "That'll do. We've got some excellent shots, and I think the problem will be choosing which one to go with."

"Excellent," Sonia said. "And that was the last of the portraits, right?"

"Yes. I just need to get some external shots of the Arts Center while the light's still good."

Axel picked his blazer off the ground. "Thanks, Hans. And thank you, Sonia. That was a lot less painful than I feared. Are you going back to the Center?"

"Yes. I've got several more things I need to do."

They walked side by side. Sonia wanted to say something, but her mind remained stubbornly blank.

Axel cleared his throat. "I was wondering whether you might want—" A shrill ring tone rang out. Axel frowned, reaching into his pocket.

Pulling out his phone, he glanced at the screen. "Oh. I'm sorry, but I have to take this call." He looked at her. "I'll catch up with you later."

He turned away, holding the phone pressed to his ear.

Sonia watched him walk back into the park, a pang of disappointment hitting her. What had he been about to ask her?

Chapter Nineteen

GLANCING AT HER WATCH, Sonia picked up her purse from her desk. There was just enough time to stop by the bakery to pick up fresh pastries before her appointment with the chairman of Berghaven's Chamber of Commerce.

Mr. Nyland had a notoriously sweet tooth, and bringing a chocolate Danish to their meeting wouldn't hurt her pitch to enlist the support of

Berghaven's business community for the Arts Center.

Her cell phone rang as she turned the door handle. Digging into her purse, she pulled out her phone. The call was from Hedwig Mikkelsen, a former business associate whom Sonia would once have considered a friend. That was before Hedwig, along with everyone else in Sonia's Trondheim social circle, went radio silent when Lauritz's downfall hit the headlines.

What could Hedwig want? Sonia checked the time. She should have left by now, but curiosity won over. She accepted the call. "Hello?"

"Hi, Sonia. How are you? It's been ages."

It certainly had. But as Sonia leaned her hip against her desk, she chose not to mention the unanswered messages and voicemails she'd left for Hedwig before moving from Trondheim. Yet. "Hi, Hedwig. What's up?"

"Lots of things. But I'm dying to hear your take on the latest news about Lauritz."

"What news?" Sonia's heart slammed against her rib cage.

"You know, the email he sent this morning."

"I don't think I got an email from Lauritz." Unless it landed in her junk mail folder, along with messages from all the other crooks. Lauritz would fit right in among the foreign princes promising millions and companies trying to sell her wonder drugs.

"Really?" Hedwig said. "He sent a press release and copied it to a bunch of his contacts. He's pleading guilty to the charges against him, and he also explicitly said you had no awareness at all about his activities. You're exonerated, Sonia."

Sonia gripped the edge of the table. "When did you hear this?"

"A couple of hours ago. Everyone I called had the same email, so I'm surprised Lauritz didn't contact you."

"That's wonderful. I don't know what to say." She sank into her chair, her hand trembling as she lifted it to her forehead. So Lauritz had some decency after all.

"I put out some feelers, and the general opinion seems to be positive toward you," Hedwig said. "Quite a few people are sympathetic because they feel you got shafted in all the initial fallout surrounding Lauritz."

Right. Where were all of these "sympathetic people," including Hedwig herself, when Sonia desperately needed a friend?

"And that's not all," Hedwig went on. "I've got the inside track on a really juicy job. They're looking for someone to help with their public relations, and now that all this Lauritz stuff is behind you, I think you'd be a perfect fit."

So, this was the real reason Hedwig was reaching out. As a corporate recruiter, she made a comfortable living headhunting candidates for high-powered roles. But although Sonia sensed it was self-interest driving Hedwig's call, she was still intrigued.

"Well, aren't you curious about the job?" Hedwig asked.

She checked the time. Unless she left right now, she wouldn't have any time to get to the bakery before her meeting. But when Hedwig continued speaking, Sonia didn't stop her.

"It's with High Stakes. Have you heard of them?"

"Of course." Which hermit hadn't heard of Europe's fastest growing online gambling chain?

"Then you know how huge they are. They're planning a major publicity push in Trondheim and want someone local to help them bring a more personable approach to their PR work. I thought of you immediately."

"I'm flattered. But I'm committed to what I'm doing here in Berghaven. I'm not planning to leave until my current project gets off the ground."

"I had a feeling you might say that," Hedwig said. "Between you and me, your work up in the boondocks is a selling point for High Stakes, because it's already marked you out as someone with whom down-to-earth people can resonate. They're very interested in you. How about I do this? I'll give them your details, no obligations at all on your part. It never hurts to make some good contacts, right?"

High Stakes, a major international player, was interested in her? The prospect soothed her battered ego. What would all the people who pretended not to know her say if she went back to Trondheim as the PR rep of High Stakes?

A strain of music spilled through her door. The choir rehearsal had started, reminding her of the time. She needed to get to her meeting. If it went well, she had a real shot at getting a significant amount of funding for the Center, which would be amazing for all the people who needed this place. And for its owner, too. An image of Axel flashed through her thoughts.

"Well, Sonia? Shall I pass on your resume and LinkedIn details to High Stakes?"

Sonia stood up and headed to the door. "Okay. No promises, though. As I said, I'm deeply invested in what I'm doing here."

"Of course, of course. No obligations."

"Thanks, Hedwig. It was great to hear from you. But I'm running late for an appointment."

"I won't keep you. All the best."

Hedwig ended the call and Sonia slung her bag over her shoulder. She would have to go straight to her meeting with Mr. Nyland. There was no time to grab the pastries now.

Chapter Twenty

Sonia looked up at the sound of knocking on her office door. "Come in."

Julie, the new lead in the musical, pushed the door open, tucking a lock of brown hair behind her ear.

Sonia smiled. Julie had been a revelation since taking over Birgitta's role. The willowy teen looked shy and unassuming, but whenever she was on stage, she transformed into a different person, one with a magnetic presence that drew every eye, and that X factor showbiz pundits liked to talk about. Sonia wouldn't be surprised if the girl one day made a career in music or acting.

"Hi. I brought this for you." Holding out a sheet of paper, Julie walked to Sonia's desk.

Sonia took the document from her. It was a release form which allowed the Center to use Julie's images in their publicity campaign. "Your mother signed this?"

Julie nodded. "Sorry, it took a while."

Sonia smiled. She'd been hounding Julie for this document for days. "Better late than never. Thank you."

"You're welcome. I'll get back to rehearsals now."

"Good. You're absolutely killing it, by the way. The show is going to be amazing."

Julie flushed as she left the office.

Sonia opened her desk, sliding the release form into a file with all the others. With Julie's parental consent secured, Sonia could go full steam ahead with her publicity campaign for the musical.

Hans's portraits of the musical's cast had turned out wonderfully. They all looked amazing in the costumes styled by Karla. But Sonia couldn't promote the musical without images of the lead actress. This consent form solved that problem.

She could now use the promo material on the Center's website, Instagram page, and other social media. Just in time, too, because they needed to build hype in the run up to opening night and, before that, the VIP preview performance. Several prominent citizens had paid premium prices to watch an early showing of the musical.

There was another knock on Sonia's door, and she smiled as Axel poked his head in.

"Hi. I know I'm a bit early for my check in, but I was in the area and

wanted to find out how things are going."

"Perfect timing. I have some excellent news to report, but first look at this."

He came around her desk so he could see her computer monitor, his clean, soapy scent and closeness filling up her space and derailing her train of thought.

"Oops, sorry. I didn't mean to close that tab. This is what I wanted to show you." She opened a series of images featuring the cast members of the musical. "I interviewed everyone who has a role in the play and wrote up profiles, and the graphics designers made these. It's all ready to go live on the Center's website."

Axel leaned forward, his face distractingly close to hers as he peered at the screen. "That looks fantastic."

"Doesn't it? And Julie just brought her signed consent form, which means we can do a publicity blitz and amp up the hype. I'm really excited about this."

He turned his gaze to her face. "I can tell."

"But wait. There's more. I met with Mr. Nyland from the Chamber of Commerce yesterday. They'll donate a full year's supply of paper, printer ink, and art supplies to the Arts Center."

The look on Axel's face filled Sonia with a warm glow. "You're a miracle worker."

"I wish I could take credit, but they believe in what the Center is doing. Mr. Nyland gave me a strong impression that the Chamber of Commerce might be open to giving a cash donation on top of that. And the board members confirmed they'll all attend our VIP preview performance, each of them paying five thousand kroner for a ticket. They'll bring their spouses, too."

Axel shook his head. "Wow. Thank God."

"The VIP show is almost sold out, and that alone should cover the dry rot and roof repairs."

"You weren't lying when you said you had excellent news." Blinking quickly, he pressed his lips together and turned away from her.

Sonia stared at him while, his back toward her, he blew out a long breath.

"Sorry. This is not exactly professional behavior." He swiped at the corner of his eye with a thumb.

Her heart swelled. "This place means a lot to you, doesn't it?"

"Yes." He faced her again. "And you've given us a lifeline. You've achieved more than I ever imagined. Thank you."

Moisture rushed to her eyes and she smiled, fanning her face with both hands. "Okay, this non-professionalism is catching."

He grinned. "I'd better find Karla. See you tomorrow."

"If not before. Lisa's out of town, but she convinced me to go to the church house group meeting tonight."

His face brightened. "She did? Then I'll see you there. Bye." He waved and left the office.

Floating on a warm cloud, Sonia turned back to her laptop. Although she'd never stopped attending Sunday services, she avoided small-group fellowships like the one that met a few streets from Lisa's home. In a more intimate setting, people were more open about their lives and struggles. She preferred the anonymity of a big service where she could wear her happy Sunday smile and nobody probed too deep about how her personal spiritual journey was going.

She spent several minutes messaging her virtual assistant, giving her the go-ahead to send out a press release and publish the new promotional material to the Center's blog and social media accounts.

She opened her LinkedIn profile to add the finishing touches to a blog post about her work in Berghaven.

There was a yawning gap since she'd removed all content relating to her work with Lauritz, so it was nice to have some current self-promo. With the Chamber of Commerce's donation and some shiny new images to use, now was the perfect time to toot her professional horn a little.

Within five minutes, her post had garnered several likes. Sonia gave a double take. One "like" had come from the marketing manager of High Stakes, the online gambling company. He'd also posted a comment.

Great seeing people working hard to lift up young people and the arts out in Norway's heartlands. Brilliant work, Sonia.

She clicked over to the man's LinkedIn profile. He'd shared her article. Wow! This day just kept getting better and better.

Chapter Twenty-One

LATER THAT EVENING, AXEL sat in his normal spot in a corner of Pastor Albert's living room. It was their regular mid-week fellowship and, as usual, they were digging deeper into the themes of the previous Sunday's sermon. But nothing else about tonight's meeting was normal.

Sonia was here.

She sat across the room on a beanbag chair, her feet tucked under her, her mere presence drawing Axel's awareness toward her like the gravitational pull of a supernova.

Everyone stood as the meeting ended, clumping into twos and threes to chat. An elderly gentleman spoke to Axel, and he repeated pleasantries on autopilot, listening with half an ear as Pastor Albert and his wife Ingrid approached Sonia a few steps away.

"It's so good to see you here, Sonia," Ingrid said. "I've seen you in church quite a few times, but it's always nice to know each other better in the house group."

Axel didn't catch Sonia's reply, because he had to focus on the man speaking to him. Finally, he ended the conversation and caught up to her as she opened the door and peered out into a steady downpour.

"Oh no, look at that. And I came here on foot."

"I can give you a ride," Axel said, whirling around as another, deeper voice echoed his offer.

Bjarne, a suave thirty-something who'd been eyeing Sonia all evening, smiled as he stepped forward. "You don't have to put yourself out, Axel. I can take Sonia home. It's on my way, but you're heading to the other side of town, right?"

Axel's face flamed. "I don't mind. It's no trouble at all."

Head tilted to one side, Sonia looked from Bjarne to Axel. She smiled at the younger man. "Thanks for the offer, Bjarne, but I'll go with Axel this time."

Axel couldn't suppress a grin as Bjarne shrugged and turned away. "I parked just down the road. I'll bring the car around if you don't mind waiting a minute."

"Let's just make a run for it," Sonia said. "Luckily, I'm wearing sensible shoes tonight."

They scurried out to his car. Rain dripping into his eyes, he held the passenger door open for her, then settled into the driver's seat.

She brushed the rain off her jacket sleeves. "Thanks for the ride. I thought it would be a good idea to get my steps in by walking this evening, and didn't think to check the forecast."

"This is Berghaven. Even if you'd checked the forecast, the weather might have decided to do something different."

She chuckled, but the drive to Lisa's house ended before he could scrape up anything clever to say or an excuse to linger.

Glancing out the window, Sonia put her hand on the door handle. After a moment, she turned back to Axel.

"Would you like to come in for some coffee?"

Coffee from Pastor Albert's wife was sloshing through his insides, but there was no way he was turning down this offer. "Thank you, if it's no trouble. Karla is staying with a friend tonight, so I can stay. I mean, not stay as in, stay over, but stay just for coffee." Served with a side of foot in mouth. Heat seared his face.

Amazingly, she didn't withdraw her offer, and he followed her into the house.

"How do you take your coffee?" she asked, putting her purse and Bible on a table.

"Black, please."

"Oh dear." She smiled, turning to face him. "That means I have to make sure it's actually good since I can't hide behind cream or sugar."

"I'm not fussy. As long as it doesn't strip paint, I'll drink it."

Laughing, she headed to the kitchen while he sat on the edge of the sofa.

She came back in a few minutes with two mugs of coffee and a plate of cookies on a tray. "Lisa made these before she went out of town. She's a genius in the kitchen."

His gaze lingered on her as she settled into the armchair with her drink. This was uncharted territory. He'd acted on impulse by coming here. She was stunning, smart, and beyond brilliant at her job. She seemed to get along well with Karla, too. But he needed to keep his attraction in check. A woman like Sonia could cause a guy to lose his head as well as his heart. With her skills, she could have her pick of jobs anywhere in the country. And her pick of men. What did he and this small town have to offer her?

Maybe if he understood more about why she'd left Berghaven, he could figure out what might keep her here.

She looked up, catching him staring.

He cleared his throat. "You told me once why you moved away from Berghaven, but you said that was the short version. What's the full story?"

She shrugged, holding his gaze for a lingering moment. "The full story is very long and pathetic. Are you sure you want to hear it?"

"I wouldn't have asked otherwise."

She put her mug on the table and tucked her feet under her. "In school, they used to call me *Fattig Sonia*. Poor Sonia."

"What? Why?"

"There were two Sonias in my first-grade class. The other Sonia was from a well-off family, but I had a single, unemployed mother with chronic health issues. Money was tight, and it showed. So, to differentiate between us, some kid came up with 'Rich

Sonia' and 'Poor Sonia,' and the name stuck."

"Kids can be cruel." He could testify to that as well.

She forced a laugh. "They could have said 'Black Sonia' and 'White Sonia'. But 'Poor Sonia' is what stuck. My mom got disability benefits, and we lived in subsidized housing. And she wasn't the best at managing money. Don't get me wrong, she did her best. But sometimes, she would blow her monthly check on a fun trip, like flying down to Kristiansand to see the zoo. We'd have an amazing week in a hotel, and then there wouldn't be enough for groceries when we got back home. One winter she bought me

a massive doll house on impulse, but my boots were a size too small."

"I'm so sorry. I had no idea."

"Then the ladies at church noticed and would help us out with groceries or hand-me-down clothes. You moved here ten years ago, so you must have met Fru Hanson before she died."

Axel nodded. Fru Hanson had been an institution in Berghaven. A wealthy widow and a pillar of the church, her charitable giving and organizational skills were legendary.

"When we came to Fru Hanson's notice, I never went hungry again. She'd go around church members' homes and collect their children's outgrown clothes and shoes and bring us bags full of groceries. Sometimes she'd rally the church ladies to come to our house and give it a thorough cleaning."

Sonia picked up an embroidered cushion, running her fingers along a line of stitches. "I know it came from a good place and it helped a lot, especially when Mom was too ill to stay on top of the chores. But I was ashamed by it all. Completely mortified. Fru Hanson would meet me in town and announce at the top of her voice how she'd be coming by tomorrow with fresh underwear or bedsheets because she'd noticed at the last cleaning session that what we had was getting threadbare. I hated it. And the kids at school..." Blinking rapidly,

she blew out a breath. "I told you it was a pathetic story."

He ached to reach out and stroke her hand.

"I'll cut it short now," she said. "Sometimes the kids at school would try to identify whose hand-me-downs I was wearing. These things stay with you. And I think deep down, all this time I've been resentful about being seen as Poor Sonia."

"I don't blame you for feeling shamed and resentful," Axel said. "And didn't Jesus say we should be discreet with our giving? The left hand should never know what the right hand has given. Generosity shouldn't be an excuse for making someone feel small."

She sat back, stroking the cushion. "Fru Hanson may have had her issues, but I can't blame her for my terrible attitude and what came out of it. I made a lot of terrible choices because I hated the thought of anyone looking down on me as a charity case. The first chance I got, I moved away from here and I applied for a credit card so I could buy my own things. And they had to be brand new and top of the line." She chuckled. "I still have a bit of a weakness for labels."

He grimaced, his mind flashing back to his own first impression of her and her designer wardrobe.

"Why the face?" she asked.

Heat flamed up his neck. "Nothing."

"No, there was something there." She leaned forward, her gaze fixed on him. "Why'd you make a face?"

He sighed. "Because I made a snap judgment when I first met you. I thought you were a flashy show-off who didn't fit in here."

"Ouch. Do you still think that?"

"Not at all."

"What do you think of me now?"

He stared into the depth of her brown eyes, his mouth going dry. As her boss, he should give her a strait-laced answer about how good she was at her job, how she had exceeded her targets and blown past all her milestones. But staring at her face, his heart full of what he'd just learned about her background, his brain refused to engage in professional mode. "I think you're the smartest, most amazing, most beautiful woman I've ever met."

Face on fire, he stared at his hands.

"Thank you." Her voice was quiet.

He looked up at her face. "After all you went through here, why did you come back to Berghaven?"

"I needed a job, and after the issues with Lauritz, this was the only place I could find one."

A weight pressed on his chest. He had his answer. But he'd always suspected she was only here because she had no other options.

"Since I came, though, I've noticed that the town has changed a lot for the better."

"Really?"

She nodded, a smile curving her lips.

"I'm—I'm really glad to hear that." He'd better ask her now before he lost his nerve and a guy like Bjarne got there first. "This may be your hometown, but a couple of new restaurants have opened since you left. Maybe you haven't had a chance to see them yet?" *Real smooth, Axel.*

With pickup lines like that, you could give Casanova a run for his money.

She laughed. "Are you asking me on a date?"

"I am. In a very ham-fisted way."

"Good thing I like ham." Her eyes twinkled. "Yes, I'd like to go out with you."

His heart racing, he pumped his fist before he could stop himself. "Awesome! Maybe dinner on Friday night?"

"Sounds good. You can take me to one of these new restaurants."

He smiled, getting to his feet. "It's late, and I'd better be going."

She stood, the motion bringing her so close to him that the warmth of her body radiated against his skin and addled his senses.

He brushed his fingers against her cheek. It was as velvety as a rose petal, just like he'd imagined. He leaned forward, hesitant, searching her face.

Her lips answered him wordlessly, soft, welcoming, and yielding as he lost himself in a lingering, intoxicating kiss.

She felt so good in his arms—too good. He needed to create some distance between them while he still could, before he did something he regretted. Stepping back, he drew in a deep breath. "I'll see you tomorrow."

Chapter Twenty-Two

SONIA SHARED A LAUGH with the journalist sitting across from her desk. The last time she'd done a media interview, it had felt like being eaten alive in a piranha tank. A completely different experience from this cozy chat with Bethany Meland from the *Berghaven Post*.

They'd known each other for close to twenty-five years, ever since they were both bridesmaids at Lisa's

wedding. Bethany, now a widow, was once married to Lisa's brother-in-law.

"We're nearly done," Bethany said, scribbling in her notepad. "Is there anything else you'd like to add that we haven't covered yet?"

Sonia tapped her chin. "Let's see." They'd gone over how members of Berghaven's business community were lining up to give their support to the Center, and how the VIP preview performance was sold out. What else should she mention? So many good things were falling into place.

The kiss she and Axel had shared last night bubbled back into her mind. She held back a grin. That was private news, not to be broadcast to the world, not even to a friendly reporter.

She pondered on Bethany's question. "Um, I would only like to add that Berghaven is in for something really special. From what I saw when I peeked in at the last rehearsal, this musical is going to make our town proud, and everyone needs to order their tickets now. We might schedule a couple of extra performances, but this is a strictly limited run. These are teens and not professionals, and they have plans for the summer. I think that's it."

Smiling, Bethany shut off her recorder. "Wonderful. I've got plenty here, and I'll run a lovely feature in the *Post* this week. I'll also make sure we

include a news piece ahead of opening night."

"Thank you so much. Every bit of publicity helps."

Bethany stowed her recorder and notebook in her tote bag. "Off the record, what's it like working with Axel Vikhammer? I wanted to interview him when he'd just bought the Center, but he turned me down flat."

"He's a great boss." And a fantastic kisser. Sonia's face warmed. "I'll see if I can talk him into giving you an interview."

"Brilliant. See you at my place this weekend? I'm looking forward to having the old gang together."

"I wouldn't miss it," Sonia said. It was weird how, since Lisa's wedding, all four bridesmaids were single, and Lisa's own marriage had broken down. But after last night's kiss with Axel, her love life was looking up. She forced her thoughts back into the present and walked Bethany out.

Her phone rang as she settled behind her desk, a number she did not recognize flashing on the screen. "Hello? This is Sonia Krogstad."

"Hi, Sonia," a deep, melodic voice said. "We've not met in person, but we've interacted online. My name is Didrik Johannson, the head of Norwegian Operations with High Stakes."

Sonia sat up straight. “Hello, Mr. Johannson. It’s nice to finally speak to you. How are you?”

“Didrik, please. I’ll cut to the chase. We’ve been following your LinkedIn profile and keeping an eye on everything you been up to. We’re very impressed with your body of work and what you’re doing right now. We want you to work with us.”

The air rushed out of Sonia’s lungs. She sucked in a quick breath. “You’re offering me a job?”

“Yes, we are. If you know anything about us, you’ll realize that making a direct offer like this is highly unusual. But we can’t imagine anyone better to head up our public relations team. We think you could bring exactly the right blend of professionalism and authenticity, and we would love to have you aboard."

"Your offer is very gratifying, but I'm not looking for a job right now."

Didrik chuckled. "We expected you to say as much, which is why we are trying our best to make our offer as hard to refuse as possible. All we ask is that you look at the terms we're proposing, and let us know in a few days whether it's worth you wrapping up your current commitments and joining us."

His confidence was palpable, even through the phone. Sonia's skin tingled. This company, worth several

billion kroner, wanted her so badly that the head of Norwegian operations was making her a direct offer. Her, Sonia, who just a few weeks ago, nobody was willing to touch with a barge pole.

All she had to do was say the word and she would be back in full force, riding higher than ever in the career she had thought was dead and buried.

She took a couple of deep breaths to focus her thoughts. “Once again, I’m very flattered by your offer. But I—”

“Don’t express your regrets just yet. Not until you’ve had a look at the email I’m sending through. Fair enough?”

She smiled. “Fair enough.”

“Excellent. Check your inbox, and I hope we’ll speak soon.”

Sonia put her phone down and clicked over to her email, where a message had just arrived from Didrik.

She opened it and clicked on the attachment, catching her breath at the very generous terms being offered. The base pay alone was more than she was making with Lauritz. And there were performance-based bonuses on top of that, which could amount to an additional fifty percent of her base pay. The retirement benefits were equally outstanding.

Didrik wasn’t lying. This was a difficult offer to refuse. She could clear her debts in no time and put

money away for the future. And what would it be like to see her old acquaintances in Trondheim with this offer in hand? Who would be laughing now?

Looking around at her small office, her gaze landed on a stack of promotional flyers for the musical. She picked one up, turning it over in her hands. The images of the youthful faces grounded her thoughts from their flight of fancy. She was committed to securing the Berghaven Arts Center's future. Her answer to Didrik would have to be a regretful no.

She clicked "reply" and typed the first words of an email to Didrik, pausing as her phone buzzed with a text message. Axel wanted to move their dinner date up to tomorrow night. A delicious warmth spread through her heart. It wasn't just the Arts Center. Berghaven had so much more to offer.

She replied Axel's text with an enthusiastic yes. Now, she had to give an equally firm "no" to Didrik.

"Sonia, do you have a minute?" Erna Vigeland, the Arts Center's director, poked her head around the door. "The promo banners have arrived and there's an issue with the sizing. It's hard to explain unless you see them. Could you have a look? We might need to send them back straight away."

Sonia glanced at her unfinished email, and back at Erna. “Sure, I’ll be right there.”

She stood up. Sorting this out might take a while, and there wasn’t enough time to give Didrik the well-worded response she needed to make. She discarded her draft email and followed Erna into the hallway.

Chapter Twenty-Three

EARLY THE NEXT MORNING, Sonia strode into the Arts Center with a garment bag over her arm. This was a two-outfit day. Her slacks and silk blouse would take her through her crazy busy work schedule and the dress rehearsal of *Freedom's Song*, and her garment bag contained a cute outfit for a late-night dinner date with Axel.

She smiled as she stepped over the worn-out flooring. The ticket sales

from tomorrow's VIP performance and the opening night for the general public would pay for the Center's most urgent renovations, including roofing, new floors, and dealing with the dry rot infestation.

She turned into the hallway leading to her office.

Erna stood in front of her door, wringing her hands.

"Sonia, I'm glad you're here. I was just about to call you. There's somebody who wants to see you urgently."

Sonia frowned. She'd come in half an hour earlier than normal, and yet Erna wanted to call her about a visitor? This must be serious. "Okay, send her through, please."

As Sonia settled behind her desk, Erna ushered a petite, birdlike woman into the room.

Erna left, closing the door behind her as the woman glared at Sonia.

Sonia gestured to a chair. "Good morning. Please have a seat. I understand you wanted to see me?"

"Are you in charge of the publicity information for the musical play?" The woman perched on the edge of the chair.

"Yes, I am. What can I do for you?"

"You could explain to me why my daughter's pictures are plastered all over the Internet."

Sonia stared at the woman. "Your daughter? Who is your daughter?"

"Julie Moen." The woman reached inside her handbag and yanked out a mobile phone, stabbing a finger at the screen until it displayed an image of the Arts Center's social media page. She thrust the phone under Sonia's nose. "Julie's pictures are all over the Internet without my consent. How did this happen?"

Sonia pushed herself backward so she could look at the phone without going cross-eyed. The Arts Center's Instagram profile was on the screen, with a portrait of a smiling Julie, the new lead actress of *Freedom's Song*.

"There must be some mistake," Sonia said. "We got signed release forms for all the minors involved in our production. Julie brought us one, too."

"That's impossible. I'm the only person with parental authority over Julie, and I would never have consented to it."

Something here was not computing. "But we do have a signed form. Sorry, what did you say your name was?"

"Bernadette Moen."

"Bear with me for a minute, Bernadette, and I'll find the form."

Swiveling her chair around, Sonia pulled open a drawer from the filing cabinet next to her desk. She located the folder with signed consent forms and extracted Julie's.

Pointing at the signature, Sonia slid the form across the desk. "Julie brought this in for us. I assure you we would never have included her in any publicity materials without seeking consent from a responsible adult in her life."

Bernadette scowled at the document. "That is not my signature."

A knot formed deep in Sonia's gut. "It's not?"

"No. Julie knows I would never have agreed to let her appear in anything so public." Breathing quickly, she crumpled into her chair. "You need to take this material down immediately. All of it."

Sonia held up her hands. She needed to calm this woman down before she began to hyperventilate. "Okay. I get that you didn't sign Julie's release form. But it might take a while to do what you're asking. Could you help me understand your concerns?"

"My concern is that my psycho ex could easily track us down because of those pictures of Julie which you've splashed all over the Internet." Bernadette's voice trembled. "We came to Berghaven to get away from him after he put me in the hospital. As soon as he was arrested, I left with

Julie. But he continued threatening us, which is why we've had to keep our whereabouts secret for the last three years. He's absolutely insane and relentless. And now you've let these pictures of her get out. He can easily find out that we're in Berghaven, and it won't take him long after that to locate us."

The knot in Sonia's gut tightened further. "I'm very sorry. We had no idea about any of this. What do you want us to do?"

"I need you to remove every scrap of content where Julie appears. Website, social media, these." She pointed at a stack of flyers on Sonia's desk. "I need all this publicity material withdrawn."

Sonia's world was spinning. She pressed her hands against her temples. "All right. I understand where you're coming from, although what you're asking is quite tricky to do since the material has already been distributed."

Bernadette leaped to her feet. "Tricky? How would you feel if you hear on the news that Julie and I were battered to death? Now, that would be tricky."

"I—"

"It seems you don't get how serious this is. I demand to see your superior. Axel Vikhammer owns the Center now, right? I want to speak to him right now."

"Yes, Axel Vikhammer owns the Center. I'll get in touch with him."

Sonia dialed Axel's number. The phone rang several times before he answered. When he did, she could hear the smile in his voice.

"Hey, Sonia. To what do I owe this delightful pleasure?"

"We have a very serious situation here at the Center. Are you able to come down to my office?"

"Of course. What's going on? Are you all right?"

"Yes, I'm fine." She glanced at Bernadette, whose eyes were fixed on her face. "I can't get into it over the phone, but you need to come here right now."

"I'll be there in ten minutes. Are you sure you're okay?"

"Yes. See you soon." Sonia ended the call and looked up at Bernadette. "He's on his way. He'll be here in ten minutes."

"Good." Bernadette stood and paced up and down the office.

"While we wait, could I offer you something to drink? A coffee, perhaps?"

"No, thank you."

They waited for ten agonizing minutes, Bernadette stalking back and forth with jerky steps. The door

opened, and Sonia held herself back from rushing into Axel's arms. Her shoulders lowered as he stepped inside, his hair still damp and stubble shading his cheeks. Her call must have caught him in the shower. Now that he was here, they could sort out this nightmare.

She stood. "Thanks for coming straight away. This is Bernadette Moen. Bernadette, this is Axel Vikhammer, the owner of the Arts Center."

"I know who you are." Bernadette ignored Axel's extended hand. "I hope you can get things happening before I involve my lawyers."

Axel looked at Sonia. "What's going on?"

Bernadette burst in before Sonia could reply. "Your publicity people have plastered my daughter Julie's picture and information all over the Internet without my consent. It's on social media and on blogs and goodness knows where else. My ex is a dangerous man and I have a restraining order against him, but that has never stopped him from coming after us before."

She dissolved into tears, hulking sobs shaking her reed-thin frame.

Axel guided Bernadette into a chair. Grabbing a tissue from Sonia's desk, he pressed it into the weeping woman's trembling hands. "I'm very sorry to hear that. Deep, steady breaths. Breathe in... and out."

Sonia watched as Bernadette followed Axel's encouragement, breathing slowly in and out as her crying subsided. His bedside manner was clearly better than Sonia's. All she'd done was rile Bernadette up further.

"Okay, let's get to the bottom of this," Axel said, pulling up a chair to sit opposite Bernadette. How did he manage to keep his voice so calm and soothing? "Your daughter's pictures have been used without your consent, and you may be in danger. First things first, we need to ensure your safety. Are you under any immediate threat?"

Bernadette shook her head. "I've been in touch with the police. Kjell is under electronic monitoring, but he's smart enough to get around it if he wants to."

"So, at least the authorities are aware. That's good. Let's see what we can do on our end." He glanced at Sonia. "How did this happen? I thought we were on top of all the consent forms."

"That's what I want to know," Bernadette said, turning her gaze on Sonia.

Sonia pointed at the form on her desk. "It appears Julie forged her mother's signature."

"What?" Axel grabbed the document and stared at it. He turned to face Bernadette. "You didn't sign this release form?"

"I categorically did not."

"I can't express how sincerely and deeply sorry we are. What can we do to make this right?"

Bernadette pointed at Sonia. "I told her that I want all the publicity materials that include Julie to be immediately taken off your website and social media accounts. She seemed to think it was too hard to do."

Axel nodded. "It is hard, but we'll do what we can. Julie and your safety has to come first."

Bernadette relaxed for the first time since she had entered Sonia's office. "Thank you. I'm glad that at least you understand the gravity of the situation. Your colleague didn't seem to take it as seriously. Now, if you'll excuse me, I have a lot to sort out."

"I'll see you out," Axel said. Without another glance at Sonia, he followed Bernadette out of the office.

Chapter Twenty-Four

As Sonia fired off an email to her virtual assistant, Axel walked back into her office.

Sinking into a chair opposite her desk, he pushed both hands through his hair. "This is an absolute nightmare."

"I know, right? I've just instructed Pamela to take our website temporarily offline and purge all Julie-related content from our social media. But there's no telling who might have shared that content from their own accounts. The flyers need canceling, as well as the printed programs. Berghaven Motors sponsored those, so we have to contact them."

Sonia groaned. "Bethany was going to publish a newspaper article tomorrow. I need to get in touch with her as well." She reached for her phone.

"How could you let this happen?"

Sonia froze. "What do you mean?"

"I mean, you were supposed to be on top of the release forms. That was the most basic part of your responsibilities."

Her hand balling into a fist, heat flushed through Sonia. "The last time I checked, my job description didn't include handwriting analysis to ensure that sixteen-year-olds aren't forging their parents' signatures."

"Sarcasm will not help us fix this."

"Neither will blaming me for something that wasn't my fault and which I couldn't have foreseen."

Their gazes locked for several moments. He sighed and held up his hands. "You're right, and I'm sorry. That was uncalled for. This wasn't your fault."

Sonia nodded, unclenching her fist. It was good that he was apologizing, but how could it have even crossed his mind to blame her? She stared at him as he stood and walked to the window. An hour ago, she'd been heading a successful fund-raising campaign and on the cusp of a new relationship. The possibilities had seemed endless. But now, the ground had shifted. Nothing felt solid anymore.

He looked out the window, arms crossed, as she left a voicemail message for Bethany, asking her friend to call her back about the feature with the *Berghaven Post*.

When Sonia put the phone down, Axel turned to face her. "How are you planning on contacting the VIP ticket holders? Will you send emails or call them individually? Calls might be better, but that'll take hours."

"Why do I need to contact them?"

He stared at her as though she'd grown a second head. "To tell them that tomorrow's VIP show is canceled. Isn't it? I didn't think you had anyone prepared to take over Julie's role."

"We don't have anyone else who can handle the role at short notice. I could ask Birgitta, but she has issues with the pitch of the songs. There was a possible solution to that, but it was something we hadn't had time to look into. And I'm not even sure whether she's in town. But why do we need to cancel the VIP performance? It's an exclusive closed event and we know exactly who'll be coming."

"There's no way Bernadette will allow Julie to take part."

Sonia closed her eyes and rubbed her temples. Was there no end to this nightmare? She looked up at Axel. "We can't cancel that show. Each of the sponsors has paid at least five thousand kroner per ticket, and several of them are considering supporting the Center long-term. I get that we may need to rethink the public performances, but the VIP showing is private, and we're counting on those funds. Surely, Bernadette can see reason."

Axel shook his head. "She is being reasonable. They're facing a genuine risk. For all we know, her ex might already be on his way to Berghaven. What if he barges in on the show?"

"That won't happen."

"But what if it does? Do you want that on your conscience? Or what if he shows up at their home? Bernadette left here getting ready to pack and leave town. That's how serious it is."

Sonia threw up her hands. "Do you know what else is serious? Our need for those funds."

"I know," he said quietly. "I'm the one who's on the hook for the money we lose, remember? But this is more important than money. We can't put a price on Julie and Bernadette's safety."

Sonia closed her mouth. With that debate-killing statement, he'd made her feel like a money-chasing mercenary for trying to salvage his fund-raising campaign. She'd taken this job to show that she could raise millions of kroner for a struggling non-profit. Was it so wrong to want to succeed? She clenched her jaw.

He glanced at his watch. "I'm sorry to take off, but I need to take care of some things, and I'm late as it is. I can free up some time if you need me to phone some people or anything like that. And, of course, you can call me if you have any questions. Otherwise, are we still on for tonight?"

She stared at him. "Tonight is off. I'll probably be sitting here all night trying to handle the fallout from all of this." She'd have to redo the publicity materials, process refunds to everyone who'd bought tickets to the show, and personally contact key sponsors.

And reconsider whether she and Axel were as compatible as she'd thought. Their date was as dead as the VIP performance, and their budding relationship might be, too.

"Okay," he said. "I'll cancel the restaurant reservation. But I could bring you a takeaway or something. You'll have to take a break and eat."

He reached out for her hand, but she pulled away, turning to yank open a desk drawer. "No, thanks. I'll be fine.

I just need to focus on dealing with this."

"Let me know if you need anything."

Out of the corner of her eye, she watched him hover for a moment before he walked out of her office.

Chapter Twenty-Five

AS THE DOOR CLOSED behind Axel, Sonia placed her palms flat on her desk and drew in a deep breath. She blew it out slowly, her eyes closed. If she was going to handle this mess, she needed to put Axel out of her mind. It was time to enter crisis mode. Thankfully, damage control was one thing she was good at. But it didn't mean she had to like it.

She spent the next half hour listing everything that needed handling in order to cancel the scheduled musical performances and remove Julie's information. Going through the list of tasks, she delegated some to her virtual assistant and a few more to Erna.

But her to-do list was still a mile long. She'd have to reach out to each sponsor. Sending emails would not do. She had to personally call everyone who'd bought a ticket to tomorrow's VIP showing or made donations towards the musical.

Opening the spreadsheet where she saved the sponsor information, she started with the first name: Mr. Nyland. The chairman of the

Berghaven Chamber of Commerce was one of the Center's most generous supporters, so it was fitting that she begin with him.

She dialed his phone number, tension twisting her gut. "Mr. Nyland? It's Sonia Krogstad from the Berghaven Community Arts Center."

"Hello, Sonia. How are you? My wife and I are looking forward to tomorrow's show."

Her grip tightened on the phone. "Actually, that's why I'm calling. I'm afraid we've had to cancel the show. One of our key cast members has a family emergency."

"I'm sorry to hear that. One of the young people, did you say? Are they okay?"

Sonia hesitated. How much information should she pass on? "The person in question is physically fine. But for reasons of personal safety involving an estranged family member, she can't take part in anything that puts her face and location out in public. Unfortunately, we only learned this after we'd gone a long way in putting the musical together."

Mr. Nyland tutted loudly. "That's a pity, but I understand your position. As long as the person is safe."

"Thank you. We'll process a refund for your tickets and, hopefully, we'll be able to set a new date for the play."

"No, no, don't worry about a refund. Consider it my family's donation to the Arts Center. And I can assure you of my continued support."

Tears pricking her eyes, Sonia pinched the bridge of her nose. She'd been prepared for a difficult conversation with tough questions and criticism. Not for such a gracious response. "Thank you," she said, her voice husky. "I appreciate that."

"Not at all. And I imagine you have a lot to handle, so I won't take up any more of your time. Chin up, young lady. You're doing a fantastic job."

Sonia ended the call. Pressing a tissue to her eyes, she allowed herself a minute to cry. And not just because he'd called her "young." She picked up the phone again and dialed the next number on the list of VIPs.

An hour and a half later, Sonia put the phone down after calling the last name on her list. She was amazed at the reactions of the VIP ticket holders she'd spoken to. When she'd explained the situation and offered a refund, all but two of them had said the Center could keep the ticket fees, expressing sympathy for Julie. Even the ones who wanted refunds had still been gracious about it.

At the very least, the Center's dry rot and roof repairs could be fixed,

taking a load of worry off her shoulders. Her fund-raising hadn't been a complete failure.

Turning back to her task list, she spent the next couple of hours working steadily through each item.

By the time she was through, the cast and supporting crew of the musical all knew the dress rehearsal and VIP show were off, to be rescheduled once somebody else was cast in the lead role.

Sitting back, she did a mental inventory of where things stood. The Center's reputation was still intact, and all their corporate sponsors said they'd stand by their financial pledges.

It looked like the morning's bombshell hadn't devastated everything after all.

A pang in her stomach reminded her she'd not eaten since breakfast. With all the immediate fires put out, she could grab a bite from the café. A late lunch or an early dinner. Not that early, since it was after five. She clicked over to her email inbox to check for anything that needed her urgent attention.

Her gaze landed on a new message from Didrik of High Stakes. He wanted to know whether she'd reconsidered his offer. Twenty-four hours ago, her response to him had been an easy no, because between her work and her love life perking up, Berghaven seemed to hold so much

for her. But now, things weren't so black and white.

Her mouse hovered over the reply button. Her fund-raising campaign would survive after Juliegate. But her relationship with Axel was a different question.

He'd been so quick to blame her for causing the crisis. And although he'd apologized straight away, he implied that she cared more about the lost funds than Julie and Bernadette's wellbeing.

Did the money matter more to her than Julie's safety? Of course not. She believed that putting on the private VIP show was an acceptable risk. But Axel thought otherwise.

She'd loved how noble and generous he was. But did she really want to be with someone so morally superior? Saint Axel of Berghaven would make her feel selfish for wanting to further her career and for thinking of things as mundane as money.

She studied Didrik's email. She had turned High Stakes down because of her commitment to see the fund-raising project through. But she'd secured several important sources of funding for the Center, setting the groundwork for future financial support. Was there still a compelling reason to say no to High Stakes?

Lisa's husband Kai. Gambling destroyed their marriage. Sonia shifted uneasily. Sure, the gambling industry

had a problematic reputation. And there were people who gambled irresponsibly, like Lisa's estranged husband. But there were also people who ate too much junk food, and that didn't make chocolate or fast food companies inherently bad.

Her mind returned to Axel standing in front of her, saying, "This is more important than money."

A sudden surge of anger flashed through her. With his successful company and his financial future secure, Axel could afford to be sanctimonious. She could not. People like him with their solid bank accounts found it easy to talk about how God provided. Her mother had relied on God's provision, too. It had come in the form of humiliating hand-me-downs from the people in her church.

She never wanted to be dependent on such provision again.

On impulse, she clicked the “reply” button on Didrik’s email and typed a message.

Your offer was too good to refuse. Thank you. I accept.

As Sonia stared at her screen, there was a knock on her door.

Axel walked in, holding a carrier bag. “I suspected you might have been

working all day, so I brought you some food. I know you said you'd be okay, but here it is, anyway."

A warm, spicy smell reached her nose. Sonia's empty gut twisted, but it wasn't because of hunger.

He stepped toward her desk. "I've got fresh naan bread, chicken korma, and rice. Are you sure I can't entice you to eat something?"

She was starving. But she couldn't bring herself to eat the food he'd brought. "That's kind of you, but no, thanks."

He looked deflated but managed a smile. "No problem. I'll leave the food here and you can eat when you're ready. How's it all going? Do you have time to give me a quick update?"

"Things are going well. Better than I expected." She summarized what she'd done and how all the sponsors were still on board, despite the show's cancellation.

"Thank God," he said. "That's wonderful news. I've been praying it would all work out."

He'd been praying, had he? She hadn't. When she prayed, everything seemed to go the opposite of how she wanted.

He put the bag down. "I'll let you get on with your work." He stepped toward the door.

"Axel, wait." He turned around and looked at her. Steeling herself, she took a deep breath. "I've decided to hand in my resignation."

His eyes widened. "What? Why?"

"I've done what I intended when I came here. I brought in several new sponsors to support the Center, and funds for the first two phases of renovation work have been fully pledged. I've still got some loose ends to tie up, but I think I'm leaving a solid foundation to build on."

He stepped forward, his gaze never leaving her face. "Is this because of the whole Julie situation?"

"Not directly." She looked away. "But it presents an opportunity to draw a line under my work here."

"I don't understand. Will you stay in Berghaven?"

It was so hard to look into his eyes. "No. I've accepted a job offer in Trondheim."

"I see." Stuffing his hands in his pockets, he paced a tight circle in the small office. "So, Berghaven, this job, all this was just a stopgap until something better came along?"

She swallowed. "My career is important to me. I've never pretended otherwise."

He looked at her for a long moment, his jaw clenched. “No, you haven’t. You said you were only here because you had no other option. Best of luck in your future endeavors. I’m sure you’ll meet great success.”

Sonia watched him leave, each step he took wrenching her heart.

Chapter Twenty-Six

SONIA ELBOWED OPEN THE front door of Lisa's house, maneuvering her way in with a large cardboard box. It contained all the personal items from her office desk. She'd accumulated a surprising amount of stuff in her stint at the Arts Center.

She headed into the living room, where Lisa lounged on the sofa watching a game show.

Lisa clicked the TV off. "What's all this? And how did the dress rehearsal go?"

Sonia dumped the box on the floor next to the coffee table. "There was no dress rehearsal. There is no musical. It's been called off."

"Why? What happened?"

Sonia kicked her shoes off and massaged a foot. "The lead actress forged her mother's consent on her release form. And it turns out, her mother has a very compelling reason for keeping herself and her daughter out of the public eye. There's a psycho ex after them, and she's worried he might track them down. Long story short, the girl's off the musical, nobody else can take the role right now, and we have to scrub all website and social media content that contains a picture or refers to her where she lives."

"Wow. What a mess. So, what's going to happen now? You said the musical's off?"

"Yes, the VIP preview is canceled, and we've postponed opening night. But that's not my problem anymore because I resigned."

Lisa held up her hand. "Whoa, hang on a minute. What am I missing? Why did you have to resign? Does Axel think it's your fault? Because I can have words with him."

"No, it's nothing like that." Sonia sighed. "It's just... I don't think it's going to work out."

"The job, or dating Axel?"

"Both."

"I still don't get it," Lisa said, frowning. "Things were going well. Then the musical gets canceled, and suddenly you're breaking up with Axel and quitting your job?"

"It's just made me think of everything in a different light. Listen, I'm exhausted and hungry, and I'd rather not talk about this."

"Okay. I guess you didn't go out to dinner either, then?"

“No. That’s why I’m starving.” Axel had left the Indian takeaway behind, but she couldn’t bring herself to eat it and had given it to the security guard at the Center.

Lisa stood. “I’ll fix you a plate.” She went into the kitchen while Sonia rubbed her aching feet.

Five minutes later, Lisa came back in, setting a tray on the dining table. “There you go.”

“Thanks.” Sonia walked to the table, inhaling the creamy carbonara sauce. This was exactly the sort of comfort food she needed. She grabbed a fork and bit into a mouthful of pasta.

Lisa watched her for a moment. "So, what comes next? Where are you going to work now?"

Sonia shifted uncomfortably. She'd been dreading this part of the conversation. "I've been offered a job back in Trondheim. With High Stakes."

Lisa went still, all expression draining from her face as she stared at Sonia.

Sonia held up her hand. "I know what you're thinking."

"Okay, tell me. What am I thinking?" Lisa's voice was quiet. A really bad sign. Lisa never shouted when she was angry. She just got silent and cold, like a frozen steel statue.

Sonia said, "With what happened with Kai, you probably have an opinion about me going to work for a gambling company. But it isn't like that. I think I can do a lot of good by helping them do projects that serve the community."

Lisa crossed her arms. "You've got to do what you've got to do, right?"

"Yes, actually, I do. I have to make a living. And High Stakes does a lot to encourage people to be responsible in their gaming. That will be a big part of my role with them."

"Are you trying to convince me, or yourself?"

"What? I'm not trying to convince anyone. I made the decision I needed

to. I've got a mountain of debt, and I'm getting nothing back from what I lost to Lauritz. I'm forty-five years old with no retirement in place, again thanks to Lauritz."

Lisa stood. "Okay. I'm going to bed."

"Lisa, wait." Sonia got to her feet and walked toward her friend. She touched Lisa's arm. "You know how sorry I am about Kai and what he put you through with his gambling. But this has nothing to do with that. I need this job, and I think I can do a lot of good with High Stakes. Please don't take it personally."

Her hands on her hips, Lisa's mouth stretched into a thin, wintry smile. "I'm trying really hard not to. But I need some time to work through this. It's...it's a lot, okay? Excuse me." Shrugging off Sonia's hand, she headed toward her bedroom.

Sonia passed a tongue over her dry lips and sank into the armchair. Her foot bumped against the box she'd brought home, filled with all her things from the Arts Center. On top of it lay the garment bag with her cute outfit. The one Axel would never see. And now it felt like she was losing her best friend, too.

But what else was she supposed to do? She was forty-five and essentially couch surfing. This job with High Stakes was her way out. She grabbed her box. It was time to pack the rest of her things.

Chapter Twenty-Seven

"Here you go, Sonia. All yours." Charlotte, the human resource manager of High Stakes, was as shiny and slick as the new corporate credit card she slid across her desk to Sonia. "Sign this form and on the back of the card, and it's all yours."

"Thank you." Sonia signed her name yet again. She'd been doing a lot of that lately, including her new contract confirming her position with High Stakes, along with a string of lucrative bonuses. Sonia Krogstad had truly arrived. This was her dream job, proof that “Poor Sonia” was dead and buried.

She passed the signed document back to Charlotte, who flashed another grin. “Thank you. We’re nearly done. I know how exhausting the onboarding process can be.”

Sonia slipped the credit card into her wallet. “There’s a lot to take in, but I’ll catch up.”

“Great. We’re all looking forward to having cocktails and dinner with you later tonight. There’s one more thing left to do for now.” Charlotte held up a

form. "This is your membership application for the Luna Club. Applying is just a formality, of course, and they'll wave your membership straight through. You can entertain guests on all Platinum Tier facilities there on the High Stakes company tab. That includes meals, massages, a golf course, pool, tennis, and squash courts. Sign here and your membership card should arrive within just a couple of days."

Sonia filled in the required information on the form. Complimentary hospitality for associates at the Luna Club? That was several steps up from taking a bag of pastries to Mr. Nyland back in Berghaven. He'd been so kind, especially his gracious reaction to the news about the musical's cancellation. What kinds of people would she be cultivating on behalf of High Stakes?

She tightened her hold on the pen and signed on the dotted line. "There you go."

"Wonderful." Charlotte beamed. "Once again, welcome to the High Stakes family. Have a great day, and I'll see you later tonight."

Sonia smiled back. "Thank you." Was the wide shiny grin an expected part of employment with High Stakes? Dental care, including veneers and tooth whitening, was part of her benefits package. She'd better start

practicing her grin if she was going to fit in.

Stepping onto the elevator, she pushed the button for the third floor. She got out, looking around to get her bearings. The offices were like a maze, if that maze were designed with luxury interiors.

She found her way back to her desk, where her immediate boss, the marketing director, stood waiting, wearing the patented High Stakes smile. Sonia mirrored it with one of her own. “Hello, Frank.”

“Hi. Charlotte told me you were on your way down, so I took the liberty of stopping by. How is your onboarding going?”

"Really well. Everyone's doing their best to help me settle in quickly."

"Excellent," Frank said. "You'll have to hit the ground running because we have a rather urgent situation that needs handling." He held up a stack of document folders and dropped them on her desk, where they landed with a dull thud. "I need you to review these materials and give me your thoughts within the next couple of hours. Specifically, I want you to think about how we will frame a press statement about the situation. The information should be in roughly chronological order, dating from when the situation began."

"All right. I'll get on it straight away," Sonia said.

"Good. When you're done, knock on my door and come in. I expect to be in all afternoon, and this is a priority." He flashed a smile at her and walked away.

Sonia settled into her chair, pulling the files toward herself. Her first official piece of work with High Stakes. Time to show them she was worth the big bucks they were paying her.

She opened the first folder, leafing through a collection of press clippings, letters, court documents, and internal memos. She studied each document, a knot of unease tightening in her gut as the picture became clearer.

The documents all involved Henrik Pederson, a man in his late thirties. In the course of his job as a warehouse employee, he suffered a brain injury. He had received a generous compensation package. He blew the entire amount, close to five million kroner, on online casinos in the space of just under one week.

After losing all the money, Mr. Pederson had sued the seven online casinos where he'd gambled away his payout, claiming he hadn't been in his right mind when he went on his gambling binge.

High Stakes owned five of the seven casinos.

The two casinos which High Stakes didn't own had settled the case out of court, agreeing to refund Mr. Pederson some of the money he'd lost on their gaming portals. However, High Stakes was digging in its heels, insisting that Mr. Pederson had spent his money legitimately. The company was taking the case all the way to trial, employing a private detective agency to dig up whatever dirt they could find on Pederson.

Sonia's assignment was to explain to the public and the media why High Stakes was refusing Henrik's claim. She had to argue that this brain injured man was responsible for his own behavior. She studied the photo of Henrik Pederson. As she stared, the round-faced Pederson faded, replaced by Lisa's estranged husband, Kai. Pederson probably had a family left distraught—first by his brain injury, and now by his gambling losses.

The compensation meant to help him cope with his brain injury was all gone. Henrik was arguing that he would never have gambled so recklessly were it not for his impaired brain. He felt the casinos should have had safeguards to prevent him from continuing to gamble.

Sonia chewed the end of her pen as she looked over her hand-written notes. High Stakes raised some strong points. Was Mr. Pederson trying to weasel out of the consequences of his own mistakes? No one had held a gun

to his head and forced him to continue gambling. And if he had ended up winning a pile of money on his binge, would he be suing High Stakes for letting him gamble?

Although she understood her employer's arguments, her conscience recoiled as though she were handling something putrid. Could she do this kind of work and still claim to have clean hands?

Her eyes fell on her newly signed contract, her salary amount standing out in bold black against the smooth white paper. Including a performance bonus, in a year she would earn roughly the compensation payout Henrik had lost in his gambling bender.

High Stakes was willing to pay her, its legal team, and a detective agency untold amounts in order to stop a mentally disabled man from getting his compensation back. There was no talk about a goodwill gesture. High Stakes wanted to win this in court. And she would be helping them. Dropping her pen onto the desk, Sonia covered her face with her hands.

Who had she become? There was nothing wrong with wanting to be financially secure. But at what cost?

She raised her head, catching a couple of her new co-workers staring at her before they glanced away. Clearing her throat, she gathered the stack of Henrik Pederson documents

and shoved them into the still-empty top drawer of her desk.

She needed somewhere quiet to think.

Five minutes later she was outside, standing in the stone-paved plaza in front of the High Stakes office. She sat on a bench, staring at an abstract fountain as it spouted showers of water that glistened in the mid-morning sunlight.

A brisk wind blew in her face. She sucked in the fresh air, but it couldn't dispel the amoral stench reeking off her new assignment. Was she really going to spin the narrative to make a billion-dollar company look good while it took money from a man with a brain injury? She would never put her career ahead of somebody else's wellbeing.

Really? What about your time at the Berghaven Community Arts Center?

Sonia sat up straight. On paper, she went to Berghaven to work for a community-based charity. But many of her decisions had been about furthering her career. Like when she'd dismissed the band and replaced the female lead. She could have found a way to include the band or tried out the transposing app so Birgitta could keep the lead role and sing for her dying grandfather.

Instead, Sonia had been focused on how the musical reflected on her, and

how she could leverage it to launch a comeback to the corporate world. And although she insisted she wasn't to blame, her actions had led to the Julie situation. Julie would never have had the lead role if Sonia hadn't insisted on it. Yes, Julie forged her mother's signature. But she was only a child who wanted her moment in the spotlight with no thought about the consequences.

And what about Lisa? Hadn't Sonia put her career ahead of her best friend's wellbeing? Lisa had opened her home and set Sonia up with a job when she desperately needed it. And in return, Sonia had turned around and started working with a gambling company, knowing full well the personal devastation gambling had brought to Lisa's life. Some friend she was.

Even without helping High Stakes against Henrik Pederson, she couldn't claim to have clean hands. Not by a long shot.

She'd been offended when Axel said some things were more important than money. Maybe she'd got upset because she knew she was putting her money first.

Axel. A knife-like pain twisted in her heart. He was the kindest, most generous-hearted man she'd ever met. But she'd left him behind, too. Choosing to chase a high-dollar, high status job with High Stakes.

Why? Why did the money matter so much to her? Because deep down, she didn't trust God to give her what she needed.

And yet he had never failed her. Her pride might have been dented because of the way God's provision came, but she'd had food and clothes growing up. And those same church community ladies whose help she resented had supported her mother in her terminal illness.

When Lauritz's business fell apart, God had, once again, provided her with a new job and a home. And the chance of a relationship with Axel.

Sonia buried her face in her hands again. Not caring who could see her, she prayed through her tears. “God, I’m so sorry. Please forgive me.”

Chapter Twenty-Eight

AXEL RAISED HIS HEAD at the sound of the front door opening and closing. Karla was home. He clicked off his stereo system, stopping a song in the middle of a plaintive chorus as her footsteps trailed up the hall. No need for her to witness her father wallowing in lovelorn power ballads from the eighties.

She dropped her bag onto the living room floor and sat cross-legged on the sofa. "What was that music?"

Axel held up a CD case. "We used to listen to these in the dark ages before Spotify. I was sorting through my music collection." More like dredging up every song he could find about heartbreak and blighted hopes. But Karla didn't have to know that. "How did your visit with Erin go?"

Karla lifted one shoulder in a shrug. "Fine, I guess. She's doing a lot better." She looked up at her father. "But she told me her family is moving to Bergen."

"Really? When will that happen?"

"Next month. Her father got a new job."

Axel processed this mixed blend of good and bad news. "He's been out of work for a while, so they must be relieved. But I can imagine how hard it will be to start afresh somewhere else."

"Yeah, I guess so." She pulled a tissue from a box in front of her, tearing it methodically into tiny shreds.

Her best friend moving away was yet another loss for Karla. He ached for his daughter, stumped over how to help her shoulder this latest blow. Should he try to comfort her? He couldn't think of anything to say that wouldn't sound lame. But maybe he didn't need to know exactly what wise words to say. Thank God she was here, sitting with him instead of isolating herself in her room.

Praying silently, he set his CD back on the shelf. He was tempted to brood in isolation and nurse his hurt after Sonia up and left. He'd fallen hard and fast for her, read too much into their relationship, and exposed too much of his heart. She'd just been passing through, while he'd wanted forever. But he would get over it. He had to. Karla needed him to be emotionally present for her.

She gathered her shredded tissue into a pile on the coffee table. "When

Erin goes, I won't have any close friends left."

"What about the people at school or at the Arts Center? Isn't there anyone there you can hang out with and get to know better?"

Karla shrugged again. "Everyone in school is part of their own clique, and I don't belong anywhere. And things at the Arts Center are weird now. We were all working so hard to get ready for the musical and when that was canceled, there was just this huge hole left. And now everyone has scattered for the summer."

She grabbed another tissue, ripping it down the middle. "I miss Sonia."

You and me both. Aloud, he sidestepped her comment. “That clique thing is the worst. I struggled with finding friends when I was around your age.”

She raised her gaze to his face. “You did?”

He didn’t want to exhume his rotten memories of what a loser he’d been back in school. But maybe Karla needed to hear about his experiences, to know that things got better. Especially with faith in God to lean on.

“I had no close friends for a really long time growing up,” he said. “Sometimes the other kids picked on me, but they mostly acted like I didn’t

exist. In some ways, being ignored was worse than the bullying. I was just a ghost. I felt that if I disappeared off the face of the earth, no one would even notice."

He winced. "It got so bad that my grandmother actually paid a bunch of kids to hang out with me."

"No way!" Karla stared at him.

"I know, right? I only found out because one of them told me. I was so happy to finally be making friends, and then I find out *Farmor* was keeping an open tab at the corner shop so these neighborhood boys could get an endless supply of comic books, soda, and candy. She meant well, but it messed me up. Killed what little self-esteem I had."

It was probably why he was so clingy and jealous when he was with Annika. Self-medicating with alcohol had only made things worse.

"So, what helped?" Karla asked. "I mean, you don't exactly have a ton of friends now, either, but you seem okay."

Axel laughed. "Thanks for the backhanded compliment."

"That came out wrong." She laughed along with him. "But, I mean, you may not have the busiest social life, but you're not Quasimodo."

He chuckled. "Quasimodo, huh? What helped?" He rubbed his chin. "I became a Christian, first of all, and learned that I matter to God. And I also learned that in order to have a genuine connection with anyone, you have to take a risk and open up. Not open up to just anyone, mind you, but it's a calculated risk. You get to know someone a bit and see if they're the kind of person you can trust and then risk showing a bit of yourself." Like telling Sonia about his past. "Sometimes it works, sometimes it doesn't. But you'll never know unless you try."

"But you don't have a girlfriend. Are you taking your own advice?"

Axel laughed. "You've got me there. Grown-ups don't have all this stuff figured out, either. We're all learning on the job. But maybe if you learn these lessons early, you can avoid some of the colossal blunders that I made."

"Do you think you made a blunder with Sonia?"

Axel stared at her, slack jawed.

Karla smiled. "I know there was something going on. I'm not blind. But then she suddenly dropped everything and left."

"I don't know whether I blundered, but I did take a risk. I guess we were just meant to be friends."

"Was it worth the risk?"

Axel thought for a moment, weighing his heart for an answer. He nodded. "It's worth the risk of getting hurt or disappointed if you know that's what it will take to make a real connection. Like when you risk lifelong humiliation by telling your daughter what a loser you were in school."

Karla giggled. "If you were a loser, then I think being a loser is pretty cool."

His throat tightened and a swell of tears blurred his vision.

She got to her feet, grabbing her bag. "I'm starving, and I don't see anything cooking. Can we have Chinese?"

He smiled. “Sure.”

Chapter Twenty-Nine

SONIA'S HEART LURCHED AT the sound of the doorbell. She was back in Berghaven, in Bethany Meland's living room.

Bethany got up from the sofa. "That must be Lisa."

As Bethany went to the front door, Sonia prayed again that God would give her the right words to say. Although she'd been waiting for this moment, she was terrified now that it was here.

Lisa came into the living room and Sonia stood, meeting her friend's gaze.

Lisa crossed her arms. "I thought you were in Trondheim."

"I'll leave the two of you to talk," Bethany said. Walking past Sonia and patting her arm, she whispered, "I'll be praying. It'll be okay."

Sonia faced Lisa. "I arrived back in town last night. I thought about calling, but I wanted to speak to you face to face." She shot a final, desperate prayer heavenward. "Lisa, I'm so sorry."

Lisa's eyes widened. "Sorry about what?"

"About going to work for High Stakes. After everything that's happened with you and Kai, I shouldn't have even considered working for a gambling company."

"Okay," Lisa said, walking farther into the room. "What's brought this on?"

"I realized just how sleazy High Stakes is and quit my job. But it should never have gone that far. I'm ashamed that it did. Can you forgive me?"

Lisa held out her arms. "Of course. Come here."

Sonia hugged her friend, relief flooding her as Lisa stroked her hair. Her financial future might be shaky, but she had her integrity and best friend back. She dabbed her eyes. “Thank you.”

“Come on.” Lisa tugged Sonia’s hand, pulling her toward the sofa. “Give me the details. What happened?”

Sonia grabbed a tissue and blew her nose as she sat. “I can’t say much because of non-disclosure stuff. But they wanted me to do something that was legal but morally shady. I thought of you and Kai and wondered how I’d got to that point, making money off the misery of gambling addicts and their families. So, I quit on the spot.”

"How did they take it?"

"They were more shocked than anything. They thought I'd lost my marbles. Thank God my contract had a probation period that allowed me to back out with no penalties."

"It took a lot of courage to quit." Lisa squeezed her hand. "But what are you going to do now? You needed that job."

Sonia shrugged. "Yes, I need a job. But for once, I believe God will open a door. He always has, even though it might be one that batters my pride to wriggle through. I'll have to tighten my belt and hang on until he does."

"I don't think they've hired anyone yet at your old job." Lisa gave Sonia a pointed look.

"No way. I can't go back there after the way I left."

"Why not?"

Because she hadn't just quit her job. She'd dumped her boss. Sonia shook her head. "Too awkward. Something else will turn up."

"Are you sticking around town?"

"For now, while I figure things out."

Lisa looked up and laughed. "Bethany's hanging around the patio door. She's probably desperate to know what's going on." She beckoned at their friend. "Come in."

Bethany pulled the door open. “Is everything okay? Did you guys make up?”

“Yes, we’re all good,” Lisa said. “Except I’m starving.”

Sonia stood. “Why don’t I get us all dinner? It’s the least I can do.”

“Thanks, but are you sure?” Lisa asked. “You need to count your pennies now that you’re jobless again.”

Sonia laughed. “If it comes to the worst, I’ll just sell my shoes on eBay. What does everyone want? Chinese?”

Chapter Thirty

AXEL WALKED INTO THE Golden Dragon Chinese restaurant in Berghaven, freezing as his gaze landed on Sonia.

Heading toward the door, she stopped mid-stride, staring wordlessly at him as her takeaway bags swung from her hands.

A nasal voice huffed behind him. “Excuse me, please.”

Realizing he was blocking the exit, Axel moved away from the door. A

wave of heat scorched its way up his face. He stepped toward Sonia, blood rushing so noisily in his ears that he spoke louder than he intended. "I didn't know you were in town."

"I haven't been here long."

"How's Trondheim? Are you settled into your new job?"

She lowered her gaze. "It didn't work out."

"That's too bad." So, that's why she was back. She was probably biding her time until another opportunity opened up. Nodding in farewell, he moved to go past her. "I need to grab my order. Karla's waiting."

Standing at the counter, he gave his details to the restaurant worker and waited for his food. Despite himself, he peeked through the corner of his eye to check whether Sonia was gone. She was still standing where he'd left her.

He gathered his bags, attempting small talk with the server, who looked past him to the next customer. Axel swung around and headed toward the door.

"Do you have a minute?" Sonia asked.

He turned to face her. "Only a minute. Like I said, Karla's waiting for her dinner."

"I know. I've got my friends' food here, too." She held up her bags. "Maybe a minute is too optimistic. But can we talk later? Please?"

A restaurant patron edged past Axel, glaring as she stepped around him. He needed to get out of the way. He looked at Sonia and nodded. "Okay. Karla's at home, though, so I can't get away tonight."

She smiled. "I'll come there in an hour."

Fifty-five minutes later, Sonia stood at Axel's front door. She deserved the cold greeting he'd given her at the restaurant. Although she'd lost his good opinion, the least she could do was apologize to him personally. She might be many things, but she wasn't a coward.

Straightening her shoulders, she pushed the doorbell.

He opened the door a few seconds later, stepping outside and pulling it shut behind him. "Hi," he said, his arms crossed.

She looked up at his face. So, he wasn't even going to ask her in. Fair enough. With Karla home, it would have been embarrassing to say what she wanted to while worrying about being overheard.

She cleared her throat. "I'll make this quick. I owe you an apology for bailing out on the Center the way I

did. When you offered me the job, you told me how important the Arts Center is, and how many people depend on it. I made a commitment to do my best, then turned around and left. I'm sorry."

His expression was unreadable, the same poker face as the day she'd first met him. "Are you hoping to get your job back?"

Heat flooding her face, she raised up her hands. "No! My goodness, no. That's not why I came here. When I got to Trondheim and started my new job, I realized... I understood my priorities were out of whack, and I was becoming the kind of person who puts financial security above everything else."

His eyebrows contracted. “Because you wanted a better-paying job?”

“It was more than that. Even when I was at the Arts Center, my chief concern was hitting fund-raising targets instead of thinking more about the people the Center was serving. And although my best friend’s marriage broke up because of her husband’s gambling addiction, I went to work for a gambling company. I had a hard talk with God when he made it clear to me what kind of person I was becoming.”

Her throat tightened. She needed to say her piece without bursting into tears. “I quit my job with the gambling company and came back to make things right with Lisa. And I’m here to

do the same thing–To apologize for leaving the Center so abruptly."

He scoured her face as though he were searching for something. Finally, he dropped his gaze. "You told me about your background and how hard you've had to struggle. I can understand why security matters to you. Thanks for letting me know. It takes a lot of moral courage to apologize."

He turned toward his door.

"That's not all."

He looked back at her, and her mouth went dry. She'd already bared her soul. She had no pride left, so she might as well go for broke. Taking a deep breath, she plunged in. "I'm not just sorry about walking out on the Center. I really regret leaving things between us the way they were."

Looking into his blue eyes made it hard to breathe.

She leaped, bracing herself for impact. "Is there an us?"

She hadn't realized she'd squeezed her eyes shut until they flew open at the touch of his palm on her cheek. Cradling her face in his hands, he laid his claim on her lips. Her heart threatened to pound its way out of her chest. She leaned into him, kissing him back, floating on a cloud of pure, wild joy.

He pulled her into his arms, holding her close to his own thudding heart as

he whispered against her hair, “Yes, Sonia. There is an us.”

Epilogue

CLOSING NIGHT OF *FREEDOM'S Song* was bittersweet. But as Sonia sat in her third-row seat, her heart soared higher than the stirring anthem the choir sang. It was impossible to be sad tonight. She had attended each performance of the musical, and it kept getting better. As with all previous showings, every seat in the auditorium of the Arts Center was occupied.

Her gaze drifted to the end of the front row, where a frail, elderly gentleman sat in a wheelchair. Although hooked up to an oxygen tank, he'd not missed a single opportunity to watch his granddaughter Birgitta in the lead role. Nils had used the transposing app to alter the key of the backing track so Birgitta could sing comfortably.

Sonia's throat tightened as the man's gnarled, bony hands moved in time to the music, as though conducting an invisible orchestra. She'd nearly robbed this family of some last precious memories. Thank God for bringing her to her senses, even though it had taken a flood—no, a tsunami—of disasters to get her attention.

Axel's arm slid around her shoulders, and Sonia's mind flew back into the present, her heart swelling with yet another reason to be thankful.

Since accepting her old job at the Arts Center, the summer and fall had flown past in a blur of work and fund-raising events. But through all the busyness, she and Axel had spent a lot of time together. Sonia couldn't believe what she'd almost allowed to slip through her fingers. He was everything her heart desired.

The dancers poured onto the stage for the musical's finale, floating like swans in Karla's beautiful costumes.

Her eyes filling, Sonia mouthed the lyrics as Birgitta and the choir sang.

Through the deep waters
And into the flood
You carried me safely,
My Father, my God
My broken heart healed,
My weakness made strong
A slave, now redeemed
I can sing freedom's song

She dabbed her eyes. There was a post-show reception for the cast and crew, and she shouldn't mess up her makeup. As the song came to an end, the audience members rose to their feet to give a spontaneous standing ovation. Clapping until her hands ached, she turned to Axel, but he wasn't beside her.

She looked back at the stage. What was this? Instead of reforming their line to take another bow, the cast members parted, Birgitta and the lead male actor unfurling an enormous banner. The audience roared and Sonia's heart pounded as the words revealed themselves in foot-high letters.

Sonia, will you marry me?

Axel walked onto the stage holding a bouquet of chrysanthemums, pansies, and asters. As the cast and

audience cheered, he looked straight at Sonia and held out his hand.

Mr. Nyland, who had the seat next to Sonia, nudged her arm. “Go on!”

Her face on fire, Sonia stepped into the aisle. She didn’t know how her feet did it, but she made it to the stage without face-planting. Giving up her makeup as a lost cause, she allowed her tears to flow freely as Axel lowered himself onto one knee.

His lips moved, the sound of his voice lost amid the deafening cheers. But she felt his words in her heart.

“I love you, Sonia. Will you be my wife?”

She nodded, sobbing as he slipped a ring onto her finger. Standing, he swept her into his arms while the crowd around them whistled, hooted, and did its best to bring the newly repaired roof down.

A second pair of arms encircled her, and Sonia looked down at Karla's dark hair.

She didn't deserve any of this. If God had allowed her to go on with her original plans, she might have been financially wealthy, but destitute in every other way. God had blessed her despite her own efforts. She was rich in grace, joy, and love.

Lisa Meland stood in the back row of the auditorium, cheering with everyone else as Axel proposed to her friend.

She'd been in on the plan, sneaking out one of Sonia's rings so Axel could tell his jeweler the correct size, and helping Karla sew the proposal banner. Although Lisa had known Axel's intentions, tears pricked her eyes as it all came together.

Sonia was a blessed woman. And Axel couldn't have chosen a wife who would love him more fiercely. She might sometimes be wrong-headed, but her huge heart was always in the right place. If anyone had a decent shot at making a marriage work, these two did.

Lisa touched the bare ring finger where her wedding band used to be. Once upon a time, she'd thought she and Kai would make it, too. But her happily ever after had collapsed like a house of cards, squandered away on the roulette tables her husband couldn't resist.

A lump formed in her throat, and bitter tears threatened to overwhelm the sweet. *No.* She would not let her heartache cloud this moment. Kai had taken enough from her. He didn't deserve any more headspace. Especially not today.

Raising her chin, she forced a wide smile and clapped louder.

Read Lisa's story in Through the Blaze, Book 2 in Milla Holt's Seasons of Faith series.

He has spent his life taking chances, but will she risk it all to love him again?

Gambling addict Kai Meland has spent the last decade fixing the life he wrecked. Still, some things are broken beyond repair. Including his marriage. His daughter's upcoming wedding might be his last chance to show his estranged wife he's not the same man who once crushed her heart by choosing gambling over her.

Lisa wants nothing to do with the man she once loved. After his addiction destroyed their family, she focused on their daughter, Eline. She wiped her tears, held her close, and met her needs. So now that Eline is about to marry, how can she want both of her parents present?

As preparations begin, Lisa finds an older, wiser Kai saying all the right things, but she's not about to fall for his charms. She's been down that road and has the scars to show it.

Will the approaching wedding allow Kai the chance he needs to break through Lisa's emotional fortress and prove to her their love is worth a final wager?

Through the Blaze is Book 2 in Milla Holt's Seasons of Faith Christian romance series. Five friends were in the same wedding in a small Norwegian town over twenty years ago. Four bridesmaids, one bride. Now, two decades on, each woman learns that God's timing is perfect as they find forever love later in life.,

About the Author

I write fiction that reflects my Christian faith. I love happy endings, heroes and heroines who discover sometimes hard but always vital truths, and stories that uplift and encourage.

My family and I live in the east of England where we enjoy rambling in the countryside, reading good books and making up silly lyrics to our favorite songs.

To learn about my other books, join my mailing list, and grab a free exclusive book, visit my website at www.millaholt.com

Made in the USA
Middletown, DE
15 July 2022

69488130R00234